"I am kr

"Your Grace should open a school for concubines!" She flamed, prey to emotions she had never felt before.

"Be careful, Athena! You are casting down the gauntlet! I never refuse a dare."

He was mocking her! The girl threw back her head to confront him face to face.

The Duke seized the opportunity. Placing his hard mouth over hers, he kissed her until she was breathless, dizzy, and stumbling. Forgotten was the crowded ballroom around them. When the Duke finally lifted his dark corsair's head from hers, Athena gasped.

She was conscious of one warm, hard hand firm against the nape of her slender neck. She was aware of a fire running along her veins, and the trembling of her knees—which seemed to be almost a permanent state when she was with the Duke. Her great golden eyes blazed up into his.

"No wonder mankind has committed every possible folly in the name of love," she said, voicing her inmost thoughts.

THE MARRIAGE MART

ELIZABETH CHATER

FAWCETT CREST • NEW YORK

Chapter 1

To say that Sir Umphrey Long was a nodcock, as his wife's mother frequently did, was perhaps too severe. His understanding was just sufficient to get him through his life as a country squire without serious entanglements or difficulties. He was a big, handsome man, universally liked for his cheerful good nature.

His wife, Dulcinia, a feather-brained female, had been as pretty as she could stare, and had had, within a month of her come-out, several flattering offers. "Fortunately," her Mama often said.

Dulcinia chose Umphrey, and had, in due course, two sturdy sons the image of their Papa, and a daughter even prettier than her Mama. The exasperated Grandmother was often heard to remark that they were all beautiful, all cheerful, and all abysmally stupid. This unnatural acerbity upon the part of so fortunate a grandparent was not resented by the good-natured Longs, who admired Lady Delia's rapier wit even when they were its target.

And then a fourth child was born, a daughter. Dulcinia, whose favorite governess had once given her a book on

Greek mythology (possibly the only book Dulcinia ever read), had intended to call her fourth child Theodora. After a few puzzled looks at the solemn little baby, she changed her mind.

"She is different," Dulcinia ventured to her doting husband and her long-suffering mother.

Umphrey took a closer look. "Well, my dear, she doesn't look like my side of the family—nor yours, for that matter," he added, assessing the thatch of black hair and the tawny-brown eyes. "Aphrodite, Achilles, and Jason have golden hair and bright blue eyes, like yours, my dearest love. They also have bigger noses and smaller mouths than this baby. But we shall love her just as dearly as though she were beautiful like Aphra and Killy and Jase," he said gently, putting a comforting large arm around her shoulders. His wife accorded him a doting smile.

His mother-in-law took a closer look at the huge, golden-brown eyes which were staring at her with the cool intensity of a well-bred kitten's. A reluctant smile tugged at Lady Delia's lips.

"I like this one," she said decidedly. "She's got presence! Possibly even brains. She looks like my father."

Umphrey and Dulcinia appeared worried, but since Lady Delia made no further comment, they were soon happy to forget the odd remark about brains.

It was only as the little girl, called Athena at her grandmother's request, grew into a quiet, intelligent young woman, that her worried parents perceived that they had produced a changeling. Where her amiable siblings had to be hauled and pushed into learning to read, write, and cipher, Athena Long could read at five, and write a legible hand at six. Her alarmed parents, nobly refusing to assign blame to the Scottish governess Lady Delia had provided, informed her ladyship of the result. The grandmother, sceptical about the reports of the prodigy, came to scoff and remained to praise the brilliance and directness of the child's mind. Athena took to learning as an eaglet takes to the shifting currents of the sky—with joyous competence.

For the next twelve years, Tina Long expanded her mind with quiet, if solitary, pleasure, while her golden siblings were very gentle with their little sister. For one thing, she didn't look like the Family. Her hair, though long and lustrous, was black and straight. Her huge golden eyes had a solemn, contemplative stare. Aphrodite whispered to her dear Mama that so much study was making poor Tina *near-sighted*, and shouldn't they do something about it?

Dulcinia sighed. She was a little ill at ease with the quiet young daughter who tended to go off into some world of her own when the rest of the Family was happily discussing important matters like hunting and new clothes and the latest interesting *on dits*. Perhaps the poor child was beginning to recognize the difference between herself and the beautiful sister and brothers?

"We must all be especially kind and loving to poor Tina," was the best Dulcinia could come up with. So they all, even Killy and Jase, did their best to compensate for their little sister's differences. Dulcinia and Aphra insisted that she accompany them on social calls to all their neighbors to drink tea and gossip; Killy and Jase wheedled her into joining them when they went out with The Hunt. And the whole Family dragged the reluctant Tina to every ball and assembly the County hostesses provided.

It was a letter from Tina, detailing some of the rigors of her social life with wry humor and a trenchant, if slightly bitter, turn of phrase, that alerted her grandmother to the dangers of the situation. She made one of her infrequent visits to the modest Long estate. Watching her granddaughter as the girl translated a poem from French into

English, Lady Delia said, with grim warning, "Your sister has just received a flattering offer from Lord Marpole."

Tina raised glorious tawny-brown eyes and smiled at her grandmother. "I am happy for Aphra. They should suit very well."

"Since Roger Marpole is eager to marry a beautiful, well-bred woman who will be easily managed, and Aphra is eager to marry, period, they should have no problems," her ladyship said tartly.

"She cares for him as much as she is able, I think," offered Tina. "And he is a kind man."

"Oh, I've no doubt they'll make a comfortable match of it. Which brings me to something I must say to you, dear child."

Athena gave her grandmother a long, considering glance. "Do not tell me you have an itch to match-make in other quarters?" she teased. "You'll catch cold at that!"

"Wretched girl," scolded her grandmother, "that is the trouble! Your—ah—fame is growing, your Mama tells me, to such an extent that it has frightened off every eligible *parti* in the county! Have you not noticed that the local youths are shy of you? I have been informed that Lawyer Cope's carrot-topped daughter Maddy was *besieged* at the last Assembly, whilst you, my poppet, sat out half the dances!"

"Closer to three quarters," Tina shrugged. "They are stupid and boring, after all."

"The Assemblies? Yes, I grant you they are, but—"

"The young men," Tina corrected her.

Her grandmother looked aghast at such plain-speaking. "Never, I repeat *never*, let such words be heard from your lips, I beg of you! To be told they are arrogant, self-willed, hard to handle, delights the Male Sex, while to have it hinted that they are philanderers or libertines quite sets them up! But to state that you find them boring and stupid will drive them away faster than the threat of the plague!" Lady Delia fluttered her elegant little fan as she contemplated her Bluestocking granddaughter with grave concern. "I see I must take you in hand. I had thought to thank Heaven that you are not a simpleton like every other member of your family, but it seems I may have been mistaken. At least they have enough *nous* to value the really *important* things—"

"Such as?" Athena's attention was fully attracted now. She was smiling that devastating, heart-catching smile which Lady Delia privately thought irresistible—and quite wasted upon one's grandparent.

"Such as Marriage—and Men," she retorted, "since we cannot have one without the other."

"Haven't you forgotten Love?" teased the girl.

"No, but I am afraid you have," riposted Lady Delia, regarding the piquant little face with a frown. After a moment she spoke again. "Have you thought of what you will be doing ten or even twenty years from now, if you continue in this fashion? Nose forever in a dusty volume, eyes straining and squinting to decipher fine print, shoulders continually bent over a desk—?"

Tina chuckled. "I'll have a dusty nose, red-rimmed eyes, and round shoulders," she suggested.

Lady Delia was not amused. "You'll be alone with your nose and your eyes and your shoulders—and no one will care what you look like in any case!"

"My family would care," objected Tina, losing a little of her amusement when presented with this undeniably gloomy picture.

"Are you content to live with those amiable moon-calves for the rest of your life? I think I know you better than that, dear child," answered Lady Delia. "You must make a life of your own. And that means marriage, for a woman of our class."

Tina frowned. "What do you suggest, Grandmama? That I attend the next Assembly and try to charm some man by flirting like Maddy Cope?"

"You would not succeed," replied her grandmother succinctly. "In the first place, you do not know how to flirt in spite of, or perhaps because of, all your erudition. In the second"—she overrode Tina's effort to interrupt—"in the second place, my poor girl, you have so terrified all the eligible young men with your learning and aloofness that you could not get near enough to any of them to flirt with him."

"You paint a dark picture," said Tina at length. "I must suppose that there are ways to overcome my handicaps, and that you have some such in mind already." She sighed. The idea of remaining at Malong Hall for the rest of her days was a daunting one. She loved her cheerful family, but had to admit that they were as stimulating intellectually as a litter of new puppies. She shook her head at the prospect. "I will do whatever you advise. I am thought to be quick to learn," she offered bravely.

Lady Delia nodded. "I believe it can be managed. But you must place yourself in my hands, girl, and you must work as you have never done before! And I must work," she added grimly. "I trust I shall be able for it."

Tina chuckled. "I would wager my blunt that you are capable of anything," she said with real admiration. "When do we start?"

"At once! First lesson: you must not use terms like 'wagering your blunt' and 'catching cold at something.' Such masculine *cant* from a young girl's lips must disgust a man of fastidious taste."

Tina frowned. "Exactly what did you have in mind for me, Grandmama? If it is to become a mealy-mouthed, niminy-piminy miss, sighing and languishing and flying up into the boughs at the slightest mention of anything interesting—!" She pulled a long face. "I could not, nor would I wish to. Better to wither on the familial vine!"

Lady Delia, who had been looking grim, unbent with a reluctant smile. "Devil!" she said affectionately, and ruffled Tina's thick silky hair with an indulgent hand. "Perhaps you are right. The worthwhile *catches* would probably scorn a prudish miss. I do have one Prize in mind, but he's been avoiding Parson's mousetrap for so long he's probably uncatchable." She sighed. "If only I were forty years younger—! Oh well, perhaps our first concern should be, as you suggest, to decide what sort of female you should be."

"I suppose I cannot just be myself?" asked Tina wistfully.

"Quite ineligible," said Lady Delia briskly. "A bluestocking, mouthing French poetry and, I have no doubt, *Latin maxims*!"

"Omnia vincit Amor?" murmured Tina naughtily. She chuckled at her grandmother's shocked expression. "It just means 'Love conquers all,' " she explained. "I thought it appropriate to our discussion."

"Just as I said!" observed Lady Delia. "Completely ruinous!"

Tina's eyes began to sparkle. "I have it! A *femme fatale*! What I believe my brothers call a Regular Dasher!"

Lady Delia rolled her eyes heavenward. "We are not seeking to establish you as some rakehell's light-o'-love, my girl!" The elderly woman was, it must be admitted, a little *in alt* at the idea of creating a New Athena who should take the Beau Monde, and one member of it in particular, by storm.

"Then if not a female pedant, nor even a *femme fatale*, will do, what role do you propose I should play?"

"How about a Woman of Mystery?" suggested Lady Delia, eyes glinting.

"Would a Man of Consequence wish to marry a Woman of Mystery? It seems unlikely to me," said Tina doubtfully. "He might be letting himself in for some unpleasant surprises."

"You are right," Lady Delia admitted. "I am permitting myself to be carried away by the—er—challenge. Make no mistake about it, my dear child, it is a challenge! Your father's estate is not such as will provide a dazzling dowry for two daughters. For one thing, he had to buy two commissions *each* for your brothers!" She frowned at Tina's gurgle of laughter.

"If you could have seen their faces when Papa came home to announce what he had done!" she chuckled. "Poor Papa intended Achilles, as the firstborn, to be the warrior, and follow in the illustrious *footsteps* of Papa's own father in the Hussars—or should I say the *horse-shoe tracks*?" She was laughing openly, her eyes alight with mirth. "I had to point out to him that Killy invariably threw out a rash when in the company of his beloved horses! The hunting season, much as he loves it, is always a wretched time for poor Killy! Then Papa admitted to us that he had planned for Jason to follow Uncle Martin into the Navy, until Jase reminded Papa of our ill-fated trip to Brighton, when a boating excursion upon even a calm ocean invariably made Jason dog-sick. Papa realized that to condemn Jase to a life at sea would be excessively cruel!"

"Your father is a widgeon," stated Lady Delia. "One would have thought, however, that even the most totty-headed of fathers would have discovered his sons' unfortunate failings before attempting to launch them upon the only careers completely impossible for them to pursue," snorted their grandmother.

"Well, he has it straightened out now," the girl soothed her. "Jason is mad about horses, and Killy seems to be enjoying his life on shipboard. All's well that ends well— as Shakespeare said."

"Shakespeare may have said it. *You* should not," criticized her grandmother. "Are you going to be sensible or not? Lacking a generous settlement, you must not flaunt your eccentricities!"

This was too much for the high-spirited girl. "I would not wish for a husband who had to be paid to take me," she said with the first anger she had shown.

"What kind of a husband *would* you like?" her grandmother asked with real interest.

Tina smiled. "An intelligent one who could talk to me about something other than hunting, gaming, and the latest mill between Prides of the Fancy." She hesitated, then continued steadily, "And one who loved me more than anything else in the world."

Lady Delia's eyebrows rose almost to her hairline.

"My poor child!" she murmured pityingly. "Your wits have been addled by all that scholarship! Don't you know that *no* persons—female at least!—of our order of Society marry for *love*?" She enunciated the word as though it were slightly obscene. "Oh, I grant you, if the woman is fortunate, a strong affection may in course of time develop. Your grandfather and I became quite good friends when he grew tired of gaming and pursuing his bits of muslin! But no member of the *Haut Ton* would admit to marrying for *love*. Quite mawkish! Absurd! Theatrical!"

"Then I must choose someone from the *Bas Ton*," retorted Tina grimly, "for I shall never marry for any other reason."

"A *Romantic*!" breathed Lady Delia with such an expression of horror that Tina was forced to laugh.

"Well, according to you and Mama, I shall never be able to get close enough to the local swains to find out whether I could love them or not! Do you dare to show your face in London with such an unlikely débutante?"

Lady Delia rose to the challenge. "I shall not only take you back with me to Portman Square, Athena, but I shall find you a suitable *parti*. And you had better be prepared to *fall in love* with him, for I warn you now, at the outset, that I do not intend to be wasting my time!"

Chapter 2

*H*is *Grace the Duke of Renfrew had not* reached his thirty-sixth year without acquiring a very good knowledge of his world and his own position in it. Even his enemies—and he had a number—were forced to admit that there was reason for the arrogance with which he depressed pretension in his inferiors. Wealthy as a nabob, a superb sportsman, darkly handsome as a corsair, more elegant than Beau Brummell, John Alexander George Stone, the Most Noble the Duke of Renfrew, was at once the challenge and the despair of every female in the Beau Monde. The fact that he quite frequently absented himself from that small and glittering company of his peers, and that few even of his intimates knew where he went, or for what purpose, served only to make him more fascinating to well-born females. The men of his own class were sure they knew—if not where he went, then certainly with what sort of companion. Such libelous *on dits* merely served to enhance His Grace's desirability.

It is also fact that His Grace had not reached his thirty-sixth year without acquiring the companionship of a small but dazzling succession of birds of paradise. Being a sensible nobleman, he had not sought his diversions among women of his own class, where matrimony was the obsessive interest. Green girls held no allure for him; and the calculated enticements to which he was subjected by fashionable matrons were enough, he often told himself, to destroy any romantic notions a man might have. He felt no need to secure the succession, since he had a nephew who was his heir. He did not like the boy over-much, and tried to see as little as possible of him and his annoying Mama, the widow of his younger brother Theodore. Lucy Stone, Dowager Countess of Bodiam, had never forgiven herself for having married the younger son. That she had not been—and never would have been—asked to marry the firstborn son did not seem to occur to her. Her manner was a combination of self-pity and envy, which made her unacceptable company for all but a few cronies and hopeful hangers-on. Even her sixteen-year-old son Harry, who had inherited, through the death of his father, the title of Earl of Bodiam, and who was the heir presumptive of his uncle the Duke, avoided his mother's company as much as possible, preferring to attend mills and cockfights with a scaff-raff company of like-minded young noblemen. Harry Stone saw as little of his daunting uncle as he could manage. This usually meant that he nerved himself for an encounter with the sophisticated and scornful Duke only when in need of financial assistance.

The Duke suffered him, as he did all fools, without pleasure, and paid only those debts which, unsettled, would have embarrassed the family name. For the rest, he adamantly refused to advance so much as a groat, and reminded Harry of his ample allowance, paid from the estate at Bodiam, and disbursed quarterly until Harry Stone should reach his majority.

His Grace the Duke was also cumbered with an older sister. Lady Sophia Rate never allowed herself or anyone else to forget that if she had been born a male, she would have been the Duke. Her two sons by her negligible husband, Sir Cecil Rate, were constantly reminded by her of their noble progenitors on the distaff side of the family. Her older son, George, who liked to be called Gogo, was a weak and sullenly envious youth who entered into all his Mama's animadversions against her younger brother the Duke, and endlessly fantasized himself holding the title. Young Nigel, and Flora, the only daughter of the house, thought their Uncle John a pretty sound apple, a regular top-o'-the-trees fellow. Flora told Nigel that there wasn't much to choose between their Mama and Lucy Stone, both of whom, she averred, were sour-tempered old jaw-me-deads. Nigel agreed, chuckling, and commiserated with the Duke, vowing it not at all strange they saw so little of him. Flora agreed.

In this opinion, Society concurred. Elegant and sophisticated ladies tittered behind their fans, murmuring that it served John Stone right to be blessed with Sophia and Lucy. The men shook their heads, asking one another how poor Stone endured it, saddled with the two most notorious shrews in the *Ton*. Through it all: attack, commiseration, mockery, the Duke bore himself with imperturbable calm, and let no one share his private counsels.

The only member of his immediate family for whom the Duke felt any degree of warmth was his nephew Nigel Rate. On the rare occasions upon which the two met, there were friendly exchanges of opinion upon the latest Pride of the Fancy, the quality of the nags up for the Derby, the probability of decent weather at Epsom Downs on the relevant days, and similar issues of importance. Their brief meetings were usually concluded by the unobtrusive passing of a comfortable handsel from uncle to nephew. After which, in perfect charity with one another, they went their separate ways.

The Duke's best—and jealous people said, his only—friend was a cheerful young nobleman named Charles Vernell. This handsome, charming, and wealthy marquess could have been the darling of London Society had he desired to be so. Instead, he seemed to prefer to accompany John Stone whenever he received the least encouragement. The Duke found so much quiet pleasure in Charles's optimistic, light-hearted company that he permitted the younger man to share most of his social activities. He even allowed him to go along on one of his frequent disappearances from London. Charles, surprised and deeply impressed at the revelation of his friend's complex nature, and the passion that burned behind the imperturbable facade which was his friend's countenance, found himself watching the dark, handsome profile as the two men drove back to London from a week spent at Renfrew Castle.

"I would never have suspected, John! The face you present to Society is so different!" The younger man shook his head, grinning.

The Duke took his eyes from the road long enough to cast a challenging look at his friend. "And exactly what face is that?"

Charles's bright blue eyes sparkled, his generous mouth curved with amusement. "Why, a very domineering, high-nosed, damn-your-eyes, arrogant phiz, to be sure! And never a hint of your—shall I say?—*other interests!* How the clubs and the boudoirs would buzz if they knew what I've just learned!"

"But you are going to say nothing," suggested his host, silkily.

Charles grinned. "Nothing—because no one would believe me! I can just hear the quizzes murmuring, 'Poor Vernell! Ripe for Bedlam! It must be the company he keeps!'" The youth's face was alight with fun. The Duke found himself grinning in sympathy.

"Ripe for Bedlam? You should have been there years ago!"

As he tooled his curricle expertly through the crowded streets of London, the Duke frowned down his aristocratic nose at the malodorous clutter, and asked himself again why he had allowed Vernell to persuade him to leave the fresh countryside for this stinking midden. If it had not been that a certain scheme of his necessitated his appearing before the House of Lords, he might well have ignored Charles's pleadings and remained at his estate, to continue those projects which currently so absorbed his interest. But there was the debate to attend, and booksellers to question.

"Is Flora to attend the Ball tonight?" Charles ventured to break the lengthy silence.

His Grace sighed. "I suppose so, She's too young, and not out yet, but the Dowager mentioned her specifically." He groaned. "Why did I permit you to remind me of the invitation? I might have avoided the wretched crush!"

"And found yourself persona non grata with the most powerful hostess in London," advised Charles. "You owe me a debt of gratitude!"

His Grace was understood to say that he knew exactly what he owed the young spoilsport, and it wasn't gratitude. Charles beguiled the rest of their journey with comments upon the charms of the new débutantes, contrasting them favorably with last season's Diamonds and Reigning Beauties. The Duke endured these eulogies with the chilly smile that depressed female pretension so effectively. At length Charles favored him with a quizzical smile.

"You're a cold fish, John! Have you never suffered a *tendre* for any female?"

"Do you think I should talk about it if I had?" queried the Duke with hauteur.

Charles had the grace to color. "No, of course not, John! Do forgive my brashness."

Renfrew unbent enough to say, quietly, "I have never met a female in whom beauty and intelligence combined in equal measure. The Sex seems to have one or the other, so that I find myself either bored by their stupidity or daunted by their ugliness."

Charles greeted this wholesale condemnation with an incredulous grin, and hastened to cite several of the Season's charmers who possessed a good measure of both wit and beauty. The Duke, however, would not allow his young friend to convince him, and found so many flaws in each lady named that Charles finally gave up with a laugh.

"None so blind as those who will not see!" he suggested.

The Duke forbore to answer, but his face showed so clearly his opinion on the matter that Charles admitted defeat, and began to discuss his chances of finding a new hunter worthy of the name at Tattersall's.

Chapter 3

At this very minute, Tina was staring at herself in a large, gilt-framed mirror in Lady Delia's comfortable Town House. She had to admit that she liked what she saw. Lady Camden's dresser had been delighted to be told to *give the child some alamodality*. It was Hugget's belief that the little country-girl could be made—under the proper guidance, which of course meant that of Hugget—into a veritable Diamond of the first water. The wily old dresser had been performing miracles with her elderly mistress for years, and fairly ached to apply her undoubted expertise upon a younger, more promising subject. She stood back now, as the awe-stricken Tina stared at her metamorphosis in the tall cheval-glass in the charming bedroom. Wonderingly, the girl breathed.

"Hugget, you are a witch! I cannot believe that this dazzling creature you have conjured up is the daunting Bluestocking who has driven all the young men away."

Hugget regarded her smugly.

"I could see the *possibilities* in you, Miss Tina—if you'll pardon the plain speaking—as soon as I clapped eyes on that hair and your figure! To say nothing of the colour of your eyes. Most unusual they are, changing to match whatever costume you put on." She bent, peering a little. "See? They're a deep gold tonight, while you're wearing that lovely yellow silk the mistress had made for you."

Tina had to admit that her eyes, huge and sparkling with the excitement of it all, were indeed a fascinating shade of tawny gold. She preened at herself, fluttering her lashes. "Effective! And I *do not* squint!" she muttered, remembering the often-expressed fears of her siblings.

Hugget pursed her lips. She, like all excellent servants, was well aware of every problem suffered by her employers, and agreed wholeheartedly with Athena's family that her stubbornly adhered-to program of study was suicidal in a young lady hopeful of conquering the *Ton.* Hugget felt obliged to issue a warning.

"Miss Tina, I have only your best interests at heart when I urge you never to mention those foreign languages you are forever reading in, and especially not that—that *book you are writing!*"

Tina flashed the woman a startled glance, then smiled, shaking her head. "I should have known better than to think I might try to bamboozle a good servant as to anything which happens in the household! Does everyone know of my—my effort?"

Hugget considered the question. "I would say, every member of the staff here at Lady Delia's establishment— possibly excepting the grooms' boy, who is deaf."

Tina digested this unwelcome intelligence in silence. "I am sure my grandmother does not know . . ." she began hesitantly.

"No, I'll warrant you she does not, else you would no longer be working upon it," conceded the dresser. "If it were even one of those frippery romances which well-born ladies divert themselves with, I should not have ventured to speak, for it is possible that some men might find it amusing in a woman that she dreams of romance—" Catching sight of Tina's offended expression, Hugget chuckled grimly. "We both know why Lady Delia brought you to London, Miss Tina, and I should think a girl of your brain power would be awake on all suits—" Hugget paused, coloring slightly under Tina's teasing glance.

" 'Awake on all suits', indeed! Better not let Lady Delia hear you mouthing *cant*, Hugget!"

The dresser sniffed and advised her charge to go to her grandmother's suite before Lady D had to send for her. "For you know, Miss Tina, her ladyship has great hopes of tonight's Ball. You would not wish to fail her, Miss, when she has done so much to make your début a success?" she urged wistfully.

"You are a slyboots, Hugget, a wily manipulator," Athena said severely, but she caught up her little reticule and the shawl of fine silk and ran lightly along the hallway to her grandmother's bedroom.

Lady Delia was waiting impatiently for her. She was, Tina admitted, impressive in black velvet and diamonds. The women scrutinized one another's costumes carefully, then shared a smile.

"We shall certainly not present a dowdy appearance at Her Grace's Ball," dimpled Tina, swishing her silk skirts in an elegant curtsey. Her shining eyes clearly revealed her pleasure in the fashionable new clothes.

"Jessica is an old martinet, but she's a clever hostess and will help me to fire you off suitably in the *Ton*," Lady Delia said. "I've known her for more years than either of us wishes to admit. You liked her granddaughter when you met her yesterday, did you not?"

"Jennifer Nairn is a darling," said Tina warmly. "She's very young, though. I shall feel like Methuselah beside her."

Lady Delia frowned thunderously. "There you go

again! Classical references can do nothing but harm to our campaign!"

"Even Biblical ones?" teased the girl.

Lady Delia set her lips. "You will promise me, Athena, before either of us sets foot outside this house, that there will be no literary comments, no political arguments, and NO speaking in foreign tongues—!"

"Except when I indicate which of the gourmet dishes I wish to sample from the buffet," teased Tina. "You will never convince me that so famous a hostess as the Dowager Duchess of Nairn employs any but a French chef!"

"You may speak of *pâtés* and *gelinottes*, although I trust you will exercise judgment in your consumption of *pâtisseries*, since we are not trying to fatten you for market—" snapped Lady Delia.

Tina could not control her laughter. "But darling Grandmama, that is exactly what you are trying to do!" she gasped.

Fuming, the old woman glared at her recalcitrant grandchild. "I despair of you," she managed, finally. "First it is an excess of scholarship, and now crude *badinage*—!"

"Oh," gasped the girl, "you are speaking in the French language, *Grandmère*! It will put all the beaux off you!"

Without another word, Lady Delia led the way past the footmen and the butler and out to the waiting carriage. But in her mind was a fierce hope that one certain nobleman, whom she most devoutly desired for her granddaughter, would be present. *Renfrew is the wiliest bachelor in London*, she thought, *but I defy even him to resist Tina in that get-up!*

Three hours later, assured of her beloved grandchild's complete acceptance by those members of the Beau Monde present at Her Grace's Ball, Lady Delia allowed herself to be persuaded to join the Dowager Duchess and

20

two elderly beaux for a refreshing game of cards in the library. The Ball was already an acknowledged success: everyone predicted that the two debutantes, Miss Athena Long and Miss Jennifer Nairn, would be Ornaments of the coming Season. For her own part, Tina was discovering that the elegant and witty London gentlemen were vastly more interesting than the rather callow young Bloods who had graced the county Assemblies. Here was rapier wit to challenge her own, and a knowledgeable attitude which put her on her mettle to hold up her side of the conversations.

Her mother had made very sure that Athena was instructed in all the social skills, so the girl had no hesitation in accepting invitations to dance. She was, indeed, rather beseiged by dapper smiling men who claimed her as a partner with gratifying alacrity. *This social life is not so dull after all*, the girl decided, sitting for a moment between dances and refreshing herself with a cup of cold, delicious punch. She was searching the room for a glimpse of her new friend, Jennifer, when her glance fell upon a massive man who was just entering the room.

Tina stared. It seemed to her that all the other men, whom she had been thinking to be so attractive, suddenly faded into commonplace before the subdued splendor of the new arrival. He was accompanied by a much younger man, a slender laughing fellow whose eyes were eagerly scanning the company. Discovering his objective, he led the older man firmly toward Jennifer Nairn. Tina felt a quite unaccustomed urge to seek out her new friend herself, so that she might be introduced to the fascinating newcomer.

In the event, this was not necessary, for great-hearted Jennifer at once led the new arrivals to meet the other débutante.

"Oh, Tina, we are so honored!" she said, a little

flustered by her awe of the older guest. "His Grace the Duke of Renfrew has come to our party, and is so eager to meet you! Your Grace, may I present Miss Athena Long? Tina, this other gentleman is Lord Charles Vernell, a—a childhood friend of mine."

"Very prettily done, minx," laughed Charles, his dark eyes smiling into those of his old friend. "Now you must promise us all the rest of the dances, for we have arrived too late to speak for ourselves."

Jennifer attempted a haughty stare and then dissolved into giggles. "Wicked creature! It would serve you right if we refused you even one single dance, coming so tardy! But for old times' sake you may have the next, which we had intended to sit out, to recover our breath. It has been such a deplorable squeeze!" Her glance roved enthusiastically over the beautifully dressed, bejewelled, laughing throng.

Charles grinned at her. "Obviously a great success! You are to be felicitated, *Jenny*!" His eyes sparkled at her look of outrage at the old nickname.

As the two old friends brangled happily, Tina was able to study the face of the big man beside her. It was a cold face, she decided, and made its owner's boredom evident. His eyes went past her to scan the crowded ballroom. He was quite obviously uninterested in the prospect of joining the crush of dancers—and equally uninterested in the young woman to whom he had just been introduced. A little flame of anger began to burn in Tina's breast. She could see no sign of the eagerness to meet her which Jennifer had mentioned. On the contrary, the wretched man had spoken exactly one word, on being presented to her: "Charmed." And looked away.

Then a cold fear blew upon Tina's anger, rousing it to a sharper response. Was her failure to charm the male sex at home to be repeated, more humiliatingly, upon this larger stage, before this more sophisticated, glittering company? At once rage shook the girl, frightening her by its intensity. *Ignore her, would he?* She spoke directly at the averted face, her voice a little high and shrill, her manner ingenuous as Jennifer's had been.

"Oh, Your Grace, you must forgive me! I have not a single dance left for you! Such a pity, is it not?" A ripple of mirth.

The big man's head turned sharply, and a pair of very disconcerting grey eyes scanned her flushed features intently. Tina bore his stare bravely, keeping the wide social smile pinned to her lips. As she took in the harsh male beauty of his dark countenance, her heart misgave her at the program she had so hastily and angrily chosen to enact, but it was too late. Jennifer and Charles were staring at her too, and the girl at least could not hide the dismay in her youthful features.

"But Tina—" she began to protest.

"Of course I must not force myself upon so popular a young débutante," said the Duke, his smile even colder and more artificial than Tina's. "If you will forgive me, Miss—er—Miss Long? I must seek out some old friends I see here." Bowing slightly, he turned and strolled away.

"I think John won that round," said Charles lightly. His bright blue eyes were kind on the girl's face, taking in its quiet beauty and the flush of embarrassment which now mantled her cheeks. "Jenny, why don't you and I join Miss Long at the buffet? You can ply me with ratafia or whatever dangerous vintages your Grandmama has provided, and you both can bring me up to date on all the London gossip."

Tina answered his well-meant gesture with the sweet smile which had so struck Lady Delia. She had no intention of playing gooseberry at the reunion of two good friends. She also felt a little faint at the icy incivility of the snub she had just received. She said, in her normal gentle voice, which was so different from the high, gushing tones she had used to the Duke, "Why thank you, My Lord, but I think I shall repair to the conservatory to snatch a moment's respite from this frenzied activity." She turned gracefully and left them before Jennifer could offer her own persuasion.

The younger girl looked at her companion ruefully. "They definitely didn't hit it off, did they?"

Lord Charles shrugged. "Renfrew's impossible. Heart of Stone. But your friend really didn't put her best foot forward, either. I suppose she was nervous at meeting the Great Man."

"Well, I don't think he's so great," fumed Jennifer, loyalty to her new friend uppermost. "He was cold and rude, and deserved to be put off! I'm going after her!"

Charles took her arm with the easy familiarity of one who had pulled her out of scrapes in her childhood. "Better leave her to nurse her wounds alone, I think," he said gently. "She seems a charming and attractive girl, when she is not endeavoring to cross swords with John Stone." At which, alas, she will undoubtedly catch a very bad cold indeed, he ruminated. He knew that closed, arrogant look which John had given the girl as he left. It was a declaration of war—a war that His Grace the Most Noble the Duke of Renfrew never lost.

As she walked swiftly into the spacious conservatory, Tina's mind was in a whirl. How could she have let that arrogant man drive her into such stupid behavior? She had less poise than the veriest adolescent! A sensible female would have made a push, at least, to charm him out of his indifference, or at least could have taken her leave of him without such a childish display! *Heaven permit that Grandmother had not witnessed the confrontation, and her own miserable part in it!* She found a seat behind a fragrant bank of flowering plants, and tried to relax in the soft light provided by groups of fairy lights.

After a few minutes, the soft splashing of the fountain, which was a central feature of the conservatory, began to work its special gentle magic upon her troubled spirits. Perhaps she could recoup the situation. Surely having offended one man would not be enough to set all Lady Delia's plans at a loss? She let her mind consider the man as she had observed him in those few tense moments. He was very large, with broad shoulders and a massive torso above well-muscled, long legs. There did not seem to be a superfluous ounce on his powerful frame. When she recalled his face, Tina felt a curious little stab that was neither fear nor anger. His Grace was such a *handsome* man, but not with the effete, soft-skinned smoothness of most of the gentlemen she had been introduced to that evening. He was hard, as though he had pushed his body to its limits of strength and endurance. And yet his garments were more elegant, if less showy, than those of most of the other male guests. Tina sighed. Definitely a man to be reckoned with—and she had dared to toss him the gauntlet! She shivered with a chill that was not quite physical. Then she pulled back into the shadows as movement near the doorway resolved itself into two male figures strolling slowly into the conservatory. She recognized the quiet voice at once.

"I shall just slip away without further ado. I have made my courtesy to our hostess, and there really isn't anyone here I care to linger for."

"You'll not go without a word to the other guest of honor, surely, John?" Charles's voice came clearly to the girl in the shadows.

"That little virago?" There was no mistaking the edge of contempt in the Duke's words.

"You forced her to it with your blasted arrogance!" his

friend protested. "Barely acknowledging the introduction, treating her with complete indifference—!"

"What else?" Renfrew came back wearily. "She is like so many of her type; pretty enough to be spoiled by young bucks with no sense of discrimination, ignorant, bad-mannered, stupid . . ." His disgust was clear in his deep tones.

"But she isn't like that at all!" protested Charles. "Jenny tells me she's quick-witted and bright, full of fun—!"

"I beg you will spare me any further details of Miss—ah—Long's girlish charms tonight," said the Duke in a voice that made Tina's hackles rise. "She is just such an one as I have always disliked—a passably pretty face with nothing behind it but vanity and malice! It is to be hoped that her sponsors will be able to catch her a husband quickly, before her charms become tarnished by her bad temper!"

With which parting shot, the Duke strolled out of the conservatory, his young friend at his shoulder still protesting.

Tina rose slowly to her feet. So that was what His Grace the Duke of Renfrew thought of Miss—ah—Long? She was actually torn between a strong desire to slap his cold, sneering face, and an equally strong wish to prove to him that she was good-tempered, intelligent, and charming. Then, catching a glimpse of her own small, clenched fists, Tina took her temper in hand and sought to regain her lost poise. When she had herself under control again, she returned to the ballroom and proceeded to captivate the younger men with a dash and sparkle that quite opened the eyes of her grandmother, come at last to check upon the progress of her fledgling. The child was a *Success*!

Whirling gaily about the huge room, Tina thought that this would prove to the arrogant peer—even *in absentia*— that she was not the poor wretch he deemed her!

Chapter 4

On the day following the Nairn Ball, the Duke set out with great reluctance to answer a querulous message from his sister, Lady Sophia. Her note had been delivered very early, but His Grace's butler had rightly decided not to trouble his master with the missive until after he had taken his breakfast. Since the Duke invariably rode for an hour before eating, this meant that the whining demand from Lady Sophia for her brother's immediate presence in her drawing room was not delivered into his hands until nearly eleven o'clock. Sighing, the Duke set out for Portland Place.

His sister was waiting for him, frozen faced. This then was to be a prolonged session, during which she would ring the changes on her grievances, disappointments, rancours, until she wore him down into agreeing with whatever scheme or demand she had in mind.

Sophia surprised him: first, by springing to the attack without preliminary skirmishing; second, by the nature of her demand.

27

"Flora must come out this Season, Renfrew. I shall need funds and your presence. I had thought we might move into the Town House."

"Impossible," stated the Duke firmly. The one thing that made his sister endurable to him was the fact that he need seldom, if ever, be in her company for more than half an hour. To make a move from the quite adequate house that Rate had provided for her, into John's own much more impressive mansion, had been her driving obsession for years. John relaxed. This was just a new move in the old battle.

Sophia surprised him again. "Flora needs a man's strong hand. She has become quite unmanageable. I cannot control her. I fear a scandal."

Fine dark eyebrows elevated above sceptical grey eyes. "You are telling me you cannot control your daughter?"

Lady Sophia brazened it out. "I am saying that the chit is completely unbiddable, headstrong, and devious to boot! For example: she informed my maid that she was going with her abigail to the Lending Library yesterday. I discovered that she had, in fact, gone into a most undesirable section of the city to purchase a ticket for—" she paused for effect— "a stage performance!"

The Duke frowned. For a well-born woman, even attended by her maid, such behavior would have been hazardous to her standing in Society. For a girl of fifteen, not yet out, the action courted disaster. Young Flora would be labelled a hoyden, hot-at-hand, perhaps worse, if the report circulated.

"You have of course told no one but myself of this?"

"Do you think me a dim-wit?" snarled Sophia. "Naturally the servants know, but perhaps if you gave them money—?"

"Is that how you secure your servants' loyalty?" asked her brother.

Lady Sophia glared at him. "I had thought you cared a little for the child! I should have realized that you hate all my children! Had I been a man, they would have been heirs to a Dukedom—!"

"Flora wouldn't," John reminded her. "As it is, your own nephew is my heir. We are both aware that you can bullock him and his silly Mama. Cannot you content yourself with that, Sophia?"

"But it may be *years*!" Anger and jealousy were removing the guards Sophia usually placed on her tongue. "And everywhere I go, I hear nothing but praises for your appearance, your wealth, your charm! And endless gossip about your romantic exploits! I live in constant fear that you will forget your obligations and marry some wretched female quite unworthy of our name!" Her voice rose.

"Enough, Sophia!" commanded her brother, striding toward the velvet bell-pull. "I shall summon your maid. You are quite overwrought. Have the child brought to me this afternoon about four. No, do not bring her yourself. Let Nigel attend her. I shall talk with her, and decide what is to be done. Perhaps you might consider removing with her to the Castle at Bodiam?" he asked hopefully. "Or to Rate's family seat?"

Sophia glared. "And leave London just as the Season is beginning? You must be joking!"

"If you are indeed so concerned over Flora's behavior, it would seem that a prolonged rustication away from the treats and temptations of the city would be beneficial," John said firmly. "I shall know better after I have talked with the girl."

Lady Sophia was so dissatisfied with the result of her attack that she let him go without further harangue.

At four o'clock that afternoon Cullon announced Miss Flora Rate and Mr. Nigel Rate.

"Bring 'em in," ordered the Duke, settling back in the chair behind his desk with a stern countenance. He was going to have to do something about Sophia—her endless whining was bad enough, but he could usually avoid listening to it. But if she intended foisting off all her problems and responsibilities upon his shoulders, he would be compelled to take charge of matters, assert his authority. He had been reluctant, for many reasons, to play the role of Head-of-the-Family, but he was, in simple truth, its head, and must accept his own responsibilities for the name's sake, if nothing else.

The two children marched in, apprehensively, obviously expecting a royal and thunderous set-down. The Duke motioned them to chairs placed in front of his desk, and sat regarding them with an impassive glance.

Nigel plucked up courage. "Hello, Uncle John," he said.

Flora, smiling nervously, echoed, "Uncle John."

The Duke fixed his eyes upon her young, flushed face.

"I am told," he said softly, "that you are displaying an interest in the theater."

"Of course Mama has tattled!" snapped the girl, going a deeper red.

"Was there any reason why she should not mention the matter?"

"It was nobody's business . . ." began the girl, mutinously. Then, at his raised eyebrow and quizzical look, she muttered, "I have nothing to do. Mama never lets me go anywhere interesting! If I have to listen to one more sour old woman babbling gossip—!"

"It does sound dull," agreed her uncle, surprisingly. "What would you wish to do?"

Flora drew a deep breath. "I would go riding in the park, attend operas, dramatic performances, balloon ascensions, races," with another deep breath, she continued, eagerly, "tour the Tower, visit Astley's Amphitheater—"

"Stop!" commanded the Duke with a grin. "You have given us enough to fill the next thirty days! Are you sure that all these delights are actually available? I seem to have lost touch with the richness of London life."

Both youngsters were staring at him incredulously.

"You don't—you *can't* mean it?" gasped Flora. "You will really take us to all these places?"

"Or see that you are taken," qualified their uncle. He scrutinized the young faces with some affection. They were, without doubt, the pick of his numerous and mostly boring relations. Perhaps he might arrange to take them to some of the entertainments Flora had mentioned. Certainly their whining, selfish mother had never bothered to put herself out for their pleasure. He rose, walked to the mantel, and pulled the bell cord.

"We shall have a good tea, and then you will go back to your home and await my summons." This rather autocratic pronouncement was softened by the warm and attractive smile that lit his face. Both young people responded to it, and the next half-hour was spent most pleasantly in eating the tasty morsels provided by His Grace's chef, and discussing the treats to come.

It did not occur to the Duke to warn Flora not to use the ticket which she had apparently purchased for the play.

Chapter 5

The London Season was rapidly gaining pace.
Night after night, rival hostesses opened their doors for all manner of exotic fêtes, ridottos, galas, grand balls, and revels. The Season bid fair to become one of the great, memorable ones in the history of the Beau Monde. Tina Long and Jennifer Nairn were deluged with invitations, sometimes attending as many as three affairs in a single evening, but Lady Delia's satisfaction was, to Tina's quick intellect, shadowed. The girl challenged her Grandmama.

"What is worrying you? Am I not *taking* well enough in the *Ton*?" She waved a thick bundle of invitations, just arrived. "I did not know there could be so many parties crowded into a few weeks' time."

Lady Delia bestowed a grim smile upon the radiant girl. "You know very well you have 'taken,' Miss! I have already fended off three separate gallants who wished to be informed of your father's address, so that they might apply for your hand. And there are two others—Dallan and Montgomery—who will find their way to Umphrey without my permission. Do you have a *tendre* for any of them, my child?"

Tina sighed. "No, Grandmama. They seemed at first to be much superior to the callow youths I met at the county Assemblies, but underneath the modish clothes and the dashing manner there is only the same boring . . . male."

Delia Camden tried to look scandalized and only succeeded in smiling. "Naughty girl! What else would you expect to find under the modish clothes? No, don't tell me! I'm sure it will be something quite shocking—or else a Latin tag!" She chuckled.

But Tina was not to be diverted. "Why do you have that shadow in your eyes, dearest Grandmama?" she persisted. "Am I doing something to embarrass you?"

Lady Delia pursed her lips. "No, child, you've provided a most interesting project, and quite enlivened these last weeks. It is—"she grimaced— "Almack's. I have not been able to wheedle any of the Patronesses into giving you a voucher! Oh, they are courteous enough, but they manage to put me off when I make even the slightest of suggestions. They are past mistresses at putting people off," she concluded waspishly.

Tina stared at her. "They do not wish me to attend their parties? But why is this? Am I not eligible by birth and behavior?"

Lady Delia uttered a sound which was almost a groan. "I managed to coax a hint out of Lady Jersey last night at the Prince's dinner. It seems that a certain nobleman has been making remarks . . ."

Tina drew herself up proudly. "About me? What could he possibly say to my detriment? Surely one does not have to have a title or a flawless beauty to receive a voucher to Almack's? Who is this noble back-stabber?"

"It is the Duke of Renfrew, drat him! You wouldn't have seen him, Tina. He dropped in at the Nairn Ball that fired you off, but apparently stayed only long enough to greet his hostess. I cannot for the life of me imagine why he should have taken you in dislike, for you've never even met the creature!" She frowned. "I will admit to you, Tina, I had hopes that your particular blending of brains and beauty would pique his interest, but it seems he has actually spoken disparagingly of you."

"On what grounds?" The girl's voice was quiet, her tone level, but her grandmother glanced up sharply. Tina's face was white—with anger? Shock? Indeed, it was a shocking thing to have ill will expressed from such a powerful source.

"It seems," admitted Lady Delia, "that he considers you to be spoiled, ignorant and bad tempered. I cannot conceive how he should have gotten such notions! It must be that he observed some other young miss behaving badly and was given your name in mistake."

"I have met His Grace," said Tina slowly. "Vernell introduced us. The Duke ignored me, and then when Vernell and Jennifer tried to force him to ask me for a dance, I—I struck back at him."

Lady Delia was regarding her with a horror-stricken expression. "You *struck back*?" she repeated faintly. "In what way?"

Tina shook her head in exasperation. "I—er—adopted a sort of high girlish voice and told him I hadn't a single dance left for him. And laughed."

Lady Delia sucked in a breath. "Laughed at him? *Fatal!*"

"He was also arrogant—so pompous and uncaring," protested Tina.

Lady Delia shivered. Then she forced a smile. This went beyond ordinary setting-to-rights. To make mock of the most powerful male figure in London society—! "My dear," she told her granddaughter, "I am quite at a stand! I do not know how to advise you."

Tina had become aware of what she had done. She had

placed her beloved grandmother in a very difficult and embarrassing position. If a débutante failed publicly, her sponsor was discredited also. Anger began to burn deep inside the girl. Why should their social success be threatened by the petty malice of one man? *I hate him!* she thought bitterly. *How carelessly he humiliates my grandmother—and destroys me!*

The older woman was speaking. "We shan't give up, of course. Invitations keep coming in, and so far, none of the leading Hostesses have blacklisted us. We shall just have to ignore Almack's. It's a dull place, and the food is beneath contempt . . ." Already her agile mind was busy with the campaign. "If anyone mentions Almack's to you, child, you must just smile prettily and say you have been *so busy accepting delightful invitations* . . . ! Finish with a delicate shrug, and then give your inquisitor that big-eyed look that young Jennifer often adopts. Conduct yourself as though Almack's was the least of your worries."

"Which it is," declared Tina stoutly. She was filled with admiration for her Machiavellian grandparent, and walked over to hug her impulsively. "You out-rival Napoleon as a Little General," she smiled lovingly. "I would back you against a dozen Dukes!"

"We haven't won yet," warned Lady Delia, but it was clear to Tina that she had pleased her grandmother. In perfect accord, the two ladies began to sort through the thick pile of invitations.

During the next few weeks it really seemed that the Beau Monde had taken Tina to its glittering heart. She danced her graceful way through several pairs of silken shoes, smiling roguishly, flirting discreetly, demurely charming the dowagers as well as the strutting males. It appeared that dark-haired Tina and honey-blonde Jennifer, enhancing foils for one another's special beauty, were becoming the darlings among the débutantes. Jennifer, who was an excellent horsewoman, soon had her own devoted coterie of admiring young gentlemen to attend her on her canters through the parks. Tina, put on her mettle by the disparaging comments of Renfrew, set out to disprove them. So successful was she that she became the most sought-after débutante on the dance floor, with all her dances promised days in advance of each ball. Lady Delia thought the chit was looking lovelier every day, and was pleased to learn that Miss Athena Long's charming yet gentle wit was much praised. Lady Delia began to hope that they might weather the Duke's disapproval after all.

And then, one day, two things happened that changed the picture completely.

Lady Delia had awakened with one of her headaches, notorious among her devoted staff. On this occasion it might have been caused by her horrified perception, the previous evening, that their only invitation for the following night was for a very boring poetry reading at the salon of a woman who wished to be known as a patroness of Literature.

"It is as I feared," she confided to her alarmed grandchild. "Everyone who counts is to attend a Gala evening at Almack's. The Prince is invited, with half a dozen other notables. Several hostesses have planned dinners beforehand for those going on to Almack's. We had better put it about that I am ill and you are unwilling to leave my bedside."

Tina tried for a joke. "You must not have anything that cannot be cured in twenty-four hours, for we are already promised to the Dowager Duchess of Nairn for tomorrow evening."

"My migraines are notorious," Lady Delia advised her. "I once failed to appear at Buckingham Palace for dinner when I had such a headache, and Their Majesties forgave me. No one will wonder at our remaining at home."

That, however, was just what Tina had no intention of doing. She had begun to find even her acknowledged success in the *Ton* a little unsatisfying, and had returned, while her Grandmother was dozing or otherwise occupied, to certain reprehensible habits of her pre-London days. Forays to the bookshops and to museums gave her stimulation of both mind and body, and she had even gotten several further chapters completed of the secret book-project that absorbed her interest. So, having been summarily dismissed by a worried Hugget from her grandparent's darkened bedroom, Tina put on a charming jade-green walking dress and a modish little hat, and, accompanied by her maid, walked down to her favorite bookstore. There she purchased a dozen volumes, of which six were novels, two of them in French. Since Lady Delia routinely discouraged any such obvious indications that her grandchild was a Bluestocking, this secret extravagance pleased Tina and set a sparkle in her fine eyes.

These eyes today had a fascinating green cast, reflected from the modish walking dress she was wearing. She stepped lightly along the pavement, dutifully followed by her maid, who was pleased to be on the strut behind so pretty a lady, and did not for a moment resent the parcel of books she carried. Driving past in his curricle, the Duke of Renfrew caught sight of the extraordinarily attractive girl, striding along so gracefully, and turned his head to watch her progress. Surely he had seen that beguiling little face before? Such open happiness was seldom displayed by the correct young women of his class.

Roused by a hoarse cry of warning, the Duke returned his glance to the road just in time to avoid a collision with a dapper man in triple-caped driving coat. Possibly stimulated by his anger at his own carelessness, the Duke suddenly recalled where he had met the girl, and the circumstances surrounding that meeting. He had, by now, come to regret the malice with which he had commented upon Miss Long to Mrs. Drummond-Burrell. It should have been beneath his dignity to strike back at the girl who was so plainly trying to depress *his* pretensions! He could chuckle at it now, in retrospect. She had been like a tiny spitting kitten, and although her voice had been shrill and her manner gushing, her fine eyes, ablaze with anger, still stayed in his memory.

Quite unaware that she had passed so close to her enemy, Tina quickly made her way back to her grandmother's home. Upon learning that Lady Delia was still laid upon her bed with Hugget in attendance, jealous of her mistress's peace and quiet, Tina said softly, "I shall not try to bother her, Hugget. I may take a drive out after dinner—in a closed carriage, of course. I am a little restless, and as there is no party to go to—"

Hugget, quite aware of the invitationless evening, merely noded understanding, and returned quietly to take up her vigil in Lady Delia's dressing room.

Tina accepted a light snack on a tray in her bedroom. Then she sent away her maid, and slipping money into her reticule, pulled on a black, hooded cape and slipped quietly downstairs while the servants were at their dinner. Smiling gently at the small page left to attend the door, she went into the street and down to the cab stand beyond the square. There she engaged a vehicle, and asked the driver to take her to the theater in which the popular comedy-drama was currently being presented.

"By Mr. Sheridan," she added hopefully. "Do you know the theater?"

"That'll be Drury Lane, Miss," the cabby said.

Tina was too much interested in all the fascinating sights of London to worry much about the gross impropriety of the step she was taking. To go unescorted to a London theater was quite beyond permission. Still, she was eager to see the performance of which she had heard so much from her partners at recent balls. If she engaged a box, and sat well back, with her hood around her head, she would surely not be recognized.

In the event, it proved impossible to engage a box, since the performance was most popular. The ticket seller did promise her that only one other person, and that another lady, occupied the box she was to share. "I shall take all the rest of the seats, then," Tina informed him. "And you are not to be pushing any more patrons in with me, sir!"

The youth grinned appreciation of her strategy, and said rather saucily that he might just be along later to make sure she was comfortable. Tina gave him a minatory glance and went to find her place.

When she reached the designated box, Tina opened the door slowly and moved into the darkened space. A girl was leaning over the rail, her attention fixed upon the crowded, loud-talking audience below her. At the sound of the door closing, this girl turned rapidly and eyed the newcomer with some alarm.

At once Tina understood what was happening. The very youthful countenance, now marred with a look of wary defiance, told her that this girl, like herself, was attending the performance without parental approval—or knowledge. The clothing was that of a much-cosseted young lady, but the elaborate black lace shawl draped over the girl's bright red hair obviously belonged to an older woman. Tina found the child's attempt to present a mature image rather pathetic. Certainly, she reminded herself, she was in no position to carp at a girl who so loved the theater that she would risk punishment to attend.

She said gently, "Good evening! I am so glad I have not missed the beginning of the play."

The tense attitude of the other girl relaxed a little, as with a gallant effort at sophistication she said, "Oh, you are in good time, ma'am! Pray be seated!" And then, blushing as she realized she need not play the hostess in a public box, she colored and turned away almost angrily.

"Thank you," said Tina gently. "This is the first time I have entered a public theater in London. I am glad to have a knowledgeable companion."

The girl turned back to her slowly, her face a little pale and her manner tentative. "Your first performance! That is an exciting moment."

Tina came toward her and took a seat near hers. She opened the cloak but did not remove the hood from her head. The younger girl watched curiously.

"Perhaps I should tell you I am thought to be taking a soothing drive in a closed carriage. I am not known to be at the theater."

The other girl's face softened into a mischievous grin. "So you are a runaway, too!" she teased, her whole pixie face bright with laughter. "My uncle would flay me alive if he knew I was here. I really wouldn't have come except that I'd already bought the ticket, and I don't have much pocket money. My Mama is a pinchpenny," she ended her random speech resentfully.

"Perhaps you'd better move back a little from the rail," Tina suggested. Her eyes had caught sight of several young male faces turned admiringly up to watch the younger girl's figure, draped over the edge of the box. "By the way, my name is Tina Long," she added, conscious of the frown on the child's face at her assumption of guidance.

Her companion, mollified, smiled back at her. "I am

Flora Rate," she offered. "Why don't you take off that cloak? You look warm."

"I do not wish to be recognized," admitted Tina. "I am in quite enough trouble already!"

Flora chuckled. The confession seemed to remove the last of the stiffness from her manner, and she sat back in her chair and turned eagerly toward Tina. Whatever she might have intended to confide was lost, however, by the raising of the curtain. Both girls settled back to enjoy the play.

By the time the first act was over, Tina decided she had never enjoyed a play more. The London actors were a different breed of beings from the weary, often inept players who toured the counties, or the amateur groups who whiled away a rain-cursed holiday with "theatricals." The girls were discussing particular parts of the play which had especially pleased them, when the door leading into the corridor was pushed open and two hard-eyed young Bucks came laughing into the box.

Tina's first impulse was to draw back into the shadows, but Flora rose to her feet, her young face flushed with excitement. The young men made their bows rather flamboyantly, Tina thought, and then addressed Flora.

"You must forgive us, pretty lady, but we thought you were . . . someone we knew."

"Oh!" Flora's disappointment was obvious. Emboldened by it, the heavier of the two men came close to her. "But that can be easily remedied, little one, can it not? That is, if we introduce ourselves, then we shall know one another!"

Flora joined in his laughter.

"I am Milton. My friend," he waved a hand, "is called Thomas. And who have we the pleasure of meeting?" He leered down at Flora.

Tina said coldly, "Whom. *Whom* have you the pleasure, etcetera. Your grammar is as offensive as your manners."

Three heads swivelled to face the grim, black-draped figure in the shadows. "Your chaperone!" said Milton sourly. "I had not noticed her."

"But she isn't!" protested Flora, disappointed at her new friend's spoil-sport attitude. "She's sneaked away from home just as I have!"

Confidence restored, Milton coaxed, "Come out and share a glass of punch with us, little one. I'm sure your friend will have no objections."

Since Flora obviously had none, Tina was in a quandary. She was certain she had never met either of the young men at any of the entertainments she had gone to with her grandmother. Still, she did not wish to draw attention to herself. How ironic if there should be someone in the theater who had met Lady Delia's granddaughter!

"I think it might be unwise, Flora," she was compelled to say. "Your uncle will flay you when he finds out."

Well, the child had said it herself. Perhaps it might be enough of a reminder to prevent Flora from committing a folly.

Indeed, the child was looking crestfallen and sober. Milton cast a disgusted look at the dark figure. "What's the harm in a glass of punch?" he protested self-righteously. Flora added her pleas. Tina began to feel like the spoil-sport Flora thought her. But she also knew that Flora had no business going anywhere with the two philanderers who were trying to scrape acquaintance. She tried to catch Flora's eye, and shook her head warningly.

But Flora was drunk with her own daring. She had actually been successful in duping her family and the servants, and getting away to the theater. Flushed with her accomplishments, she longed for the further excitement of drinking punch with two flattering male companions. She held out one hand to Milton. "I'll go with you!"

"That's the barber!" grinned Milton. "Coming, Tom?"

The other man shrugged. "Might as well. There's no sport in this pious bitch."

Flora hesitated, offended at his crudity to her new friend. "Will you not join us, Tina? I am sure you must be as thirsty as I am, after all the laughing we did."

"I wish you would reconsider, Flora," she urged. A wicked scheme presented itself to her. "You recall how your uncle acted the last time he caught you with a strange young man?"

Three pairs of eyes flashed to her face. Flora frowned in bewilderment. "But he—" she began to object.

Milton, not so sure now of the wisdom of his behavior, blustered, " 'Tis only to drink a glass of punch in a public place. There'll be half of London in the lobby to chaperone us."

This idea was naturally distasteful to the girl who was absent without leave from her home. She closed her mouth and looked from Tina to the men.

Thomas, less aggressive than his friend, was also having second thoughts. If the forward little piece was really Somebody, or had a fire-eating relative—! It seemed to him wiser to be off to easier, less dangerous, conquests.

Tina observed his dampened enthusiasm with relish. Feeling stimulated by the play-acting, she embroidered her tale. "Why, Mr. Thomas," she said sweetly, "a very dashing young blade, somewhat of your appearance, tried to cast out lures to Flora in the Pump Room in Bath. My friend's uncle hired two bravos to accost the hapless fellow on his way to his rooms that evening. They battered the poor wretch into insensibility. But I am sure you will not let that prospect daunt you."

43

Thomas was already easing himself out of the box. Milton cast a resentful look at the older girl. "Of course I would not—if I were fool enough to believe you. But it is almost time for the interval to end, and we must return to our seats. Thanks to your bloody interference, your friend has lost the chance to refresh herself!" With this petulant protest, Milton swept Flora an ostentatious bow, glared at Tina, and followed his friend from the box.

"Now see what you have done!" wailed Flora, dissolving into tears.

Tina led her, crying, to a chair away from the railing.

"Who is that lady in the opposite box?" she asked ingenuously. "She seems to think she knows you, Flora."

At once the girl stopped crying and huddled back against Tina. "Oh, I dare not look! Who is it? Do you recognize her?"

"No," admitted Tina with perfect honesty. The woman had not even glanced in their direction, but the ploy had been a good one. Flora was by now thoroughly frightened out of her tantrum, and turned her tear-stained face pathetically toward the older girl.

"I think I had better go home," she whispered. "I have spoilt the evening for us both."

"Indeed you have not," said Tina gently. "It was those encroaching fellows who spoiled it, Flora. A shab-rag couple, with more hair than wit, as my brother Killy would say. But you can rest assured that they will not dare return to pester us! Shall we try to enjoy the rest of the play?"

"Lady Teazle, Lady Teazle, I'll not bear it!" came the voice of the actor who played Sir Peter. The audience was intent upon the stage. Flora, however, had taken fright. The unpleasant scene played out in the box was a far cry from her adolescent fantasies, and had quite destroyed

her pleasure in her stolen outing. She was beginning to realize that she had been saved from a disastrous situation by the good offices of her new friend. She insisted on leaving the theater while everyone was absorbed in the play.

Tina, who had been enjoying Mr. Sheridan's wit, was reluctant to leave in mid-scene, as it were. Still, she found herself even more unwilling to let the wilful child make her own precarious way out of the theater and home. She drew a deep breath of frustration, staring down into the tear-streaked, childish countenance. Did no one care about the girl? Was there no mother to see that she had enough activities suitable for her age to keep her from yearning after these forbidden treats? And this uncle who was so unfeeling—would he not be better escorting the child to some of the functions which might be at once interesting and relatively innocent? Men were such selfish creatures! Her angry disapproval of Flora's heartless family prodded her into going with the girl to see her safely home.

Since the play was still in progress, there was no difficulty in securing a hackney to take them to Flora's residence. The girl, subdued and nervous, gave Tina her address in a low voice, and clung to the older girl's hand all the way to the oppressively elegant mansion.

Tina smiled encouragingly at her as the cabby opened the door. "So, my dear, you are safely arrived! You will do very well from now on, I feel sure."

Flora refused to release Tina's hand. "I do not know how to thank you," she muttered.

Tina pressed her fingers lightly and said with a warm smile, "If you mean that, I can soon tell you how to reward me for whatever little service I may have performed. Will you promise me that you will not again creep away to the theater without some member of your family or an older friend in attendance? It is really much more pleasant to share the delights of the play with a kindred spirit, you know."

Flora slanted a mischievous grin under long lashes. "I have found that to be fact! Thanks to your story of the battered betrayer, those two wretches showed their true colors!" She giggled. "Oh, how I wish *you* were my friend! My life is so dull and—and *lonely*! You made it all so jolly!"

Tina tried to bring the leavetaking to an end. She was sorry for the pretty child, but quite understood how little a chance-met stranger could do to relieve her boredom and loneliness. She said, lightly, "It was really very wicked of me to tell those creatures such a whisker about your uncle. I am sure the poor man never hired a bully in his life."

The cabby, standing by the door, gave them a sour glance. "Be ye ladies plannin' to spend the night in there?" he asked.

Flora's clutch tightened.

"Uncle John would have no need to hire bullies," she said. "He is a notable exponent of the art of fisticuffs, and would be quite able to mill those villains down without aid! But I loved your story. It was so—exciting!" She pulled at Tina's hand. "Oh, do come in with me! We can have tea—or a glass of ratafia—at least, *you* can," she added. "I am not permitted to indulge in it yet. Oh, do say you will come in with me!"

Correctly estimating that the urgency behind the invitation rose in great part from Flora's reluctance to enter her home alone, Tina sighed and preceded her out of the hackney. Paying off the driver, she smiled at Flora.

"Yes, thank you, I will come in with you. I owe you something for promising me not to go unattended to the theater, do I not?"

Thankfully, Flora led the way up the massive steps and plied the knocker so softly Tina feared no one would hear it. To her surprise, the great door swung open almost before Flora's hand left the kocker. A stern-faced butler frowned down upon the two girls, then stood back and waved them into the hallway.

"Where have you been, Miss Flora? Her Ladyship is most annoyed! Come this way at once, if you please!" No courtesy for Flora's guest.

Flora had deflated into a miserable posture. Gone was the air of sparkling mischief with which she had greeted the intruders in the box at the theater. Gone even the wide-eyed, pathetic little figure who had pleaded with Tina in the hackney. This was a girl going to torment, dumbly accepting punishment she knew she could not avoid. Something in Tina rebelled against the transformation—or rather, against those who had so effortlessly effected it.

"I shall come with you, my dear Flora," she said in her most haughty voice. She glanced arrogantly at the shocked servant. "It is to be hoped that I shall be received with more civility in the drawing room than I have encountered in this hallway."

She threw back the dark hood, revealing her small beautiful face crowned in gleaming black hair and illumined by the huge brown eyes now blazing magnificently. The butler was stunned by her regal appearance as much as by her words of criticism. Even Flora looked up at her new friend, the faintest flicker of hope in her frightened countenance.

Tina waved a hand at the butler. Completely subdued, Groat turned and led the way up the wide stairs, past the ostentatious gold frames enshrining the noble ancestors of this small, forlorn child beside her, now clinging desperately to her hand. What had they done to the girl, this family of hers? Tina had been used to a good deal of cosseting from her own, amiable, family and was truly shocked to observe the behavior of a girl who was reduced to mute terror at the prospect of meeting her Mama. With every step she took up the carpeted stairway, Tina's sense of outrage increased. Her reading, wide-ranging through several languages and as many centuries, had prepared her to accept the idea of cruel parents and innocent young victims. Had not Agamemnon sacrificed his daughter Iphigenia to the goddess to appease some gods the father himself had insulted? Had not Creon ordered that Antigone, his own son's fiancée, be buried alive? Had not Medea murdered her two children? By the time Tina reached the drawing room, she had recalled Juliet and the cruel insensitivity of *her* parents. She swept into the ornately furnished chamber prepared to do battle for poor Flora.

Her somewhat tempestuous entrance was observed and then ignored contemptuously by the middle-aged, high-nosed dame on a satin chair by the meager fire.

It is no wonder the child looks pinched! This place has the chill of a dungeon, thought Tina wrathfully. *Flora is denied physical warmth as well as love!* She put an arm around the shrinking girl.

The older woman, dressed in an elaborate but unbecoming gown, spoke coldly to her daughter. "This latest example of irresponsible behavior upon your part, Flora, has confirmed my judgment. You will return to the country tomorrow morning, before you can disgrace the Family." She shook her head at her daughter's cry of anguish. "Do not offer excuses. I have no wish to know in what squalid surroundings you have been amusing yourself, nor with what ill-bred companions."

"My breeding is obviously different from your own, Milady," said Tina, carried away from prudence at the sight of Flora's white, strained face. "In my parents' home, a guest is treated with courtesy, and a daughter is given a loving hearing before summary judgment is pronounced! The poet Blake truly says: 'Cruelty has a human heart'!"

Lady Sophia was goggling at this impertinent setdown, when a deep, amused male voice spoke from behind Tina. "God help us, a Bluestocking!" Tina whirled and felt her heart jar in her breast at sight of the tall, powerful man who stood just inside the open doorway, regarding the three women with a sardonic smile. It was the arrogant, hateful Duke of Renfrew! Tina drew a deep breath, more than ever ready to fly to the defence of a girl who had this monster for a relative. But before she could frame her attack, the man looked beyond her to the angry woman upon the chair.

"These young ladies have been attending a very proper—and I am sure, boring—reading of verse at the home of Lady . . ." He paused as though trying to recollect the name of their hostess, and his challenging stare mocked Tina.

"Lady Teazle," Tina supplied composedly. "And the—readings were far from boring." Let him handle that one, the arrogant devil!

"I suppose it is all a matter of taste," acknowledged the devil, with a grin that set her nerve-endings to tingling. "If you had proceeded with the least modicum of tact, my dear Sophia, you would have discovered that this lady who accompanied your daughter this evening is Miss Athena Long, a well-known scholar and granddaughter of Lady Cordelia Camden. She and the Dowager Duchess of Nairn are firing off their débutantes this Season."

"I have not seen either of them at Almack's," objected Lady Sophia, scrutinizing Tina with a jaundiced air.

"I am afraid Miss Long is *too busy* with her studies to

care for dancing—or so I have been led to believe," and his smile at Tina was as cruel as his words had been in the conservatory.

"Does Lady Camden permit you to go unescorted to *soirées*?" Lady Sophia pursued relentlessly. "And why did you, Flora, fail to inform your maid as to your destination when you went out? The stupid girl did not seem to know anything of your plans when I questioned her!"

Renfrew laughed. "But then you have such formidable manner when you are questioning anyone, my dear Sophia! Perhaps you frightened the poor female into speechlessness?"

Lady Sophia glared at her brother. Tina could see that there was no love lost between the pair. She hated the Duke, of course; but he had intervened with a wily suggestion in a moment of stress, and Tina decided to use him as an ally to help poor Flora.

"Her Ladyship spoke of you tonight, Your Grace," she smiled complacently. "She said you—"

The Duke held up one strong, lean hand. "Spare my blushes," he intoned, his eyes bright and predatory, "or I shall have to tell everyone what she said of you, Miss Long."

It was a warning, clearly. Tina stared at the mocking face for a moment and then backed down. "It was flattering," she advised him, and he laughed shortly.

His sister regarded the two suspiciously. "You know this girl well, Renfrew?" she queried.

"I was introduced to Miss Long at the Nairn Ball. We have met a few times since." His air was off-hand, discouraging comment.

Lady Sophia was never content to let well enough alone. "I had not realized you had literary pretensions, John," she sneered.

Tina was seized by an irresistible urge. "But Lady

50

Sophia, His Grace's triplets are famous, and his sonnets quite bring me to raptures!" She sighed theatrically, and rolled her eyes heavenward.

To her surprise, the Duke threw back his handsome head and laughed heartily. Then, sobering under his sister's vitriolic stare, he said smugly, "I am flattered to have made such an impression upon you, Miss Long."

Drat the man, fumed Tina. He knew what he had said about her—and also that he had scotched her chances for a voucher for Almack's. Suddenly all the fun drained out of her, and Tina wanted nothing more than to leave this maddening man and his cruel sister and seek sanctuary in her grandmother's home. She turned and made a graceful curtsey to Flora's mother.

"Now that I have seen Flora safely home to you, Milady, I must take my leave. My grandmother will be waiting to hear about the—the reading."

Lady Sophia gave a grudging nod, and Flora thankfully escorted her new friend out into the wide hallway and down the stairs. As they left, both girls heard Lady Sophia's suspicious voice saying, "I have not heard of a Lady Teazle, Renfrew! There is the dowdy Gracelle female who is forever rambling on about poets, but she—"

"They are all beyond your notice, Sophia," the Duke's deep voice came to the girls. "I advise you to forget it."

"I would not have Flora turning into a female pedant!" snapped his sister.

The girls hurried on down the stairs.

"How will you get home?" whispered Flora. "Shall I ask Groat to summon a hackney?"

"That will be unnecessary," the Duke's voice advised them.

"How did you get here?" Flora cried out. "You are upstairs talking to Mama!"

"I am?" queried the Duke silkily. "And I thought I was about to drive Miss Athena Long back to her grandmother's house. For you must know that I could not permit her to try to find a hackney at this hour. Not even a Bluestocking could survive the scandal if it came out that she was roaming the streets unescorted at midnight!"

Both girls were forced to admit the truth of this. Flora hastily kissed Tina on the cheek, pressed her hand in a speaking manner, and fled back up the stairs.

"Silly little chit," muttered the Duke, and offered his arm to Tina.

As Groat was at this moment opening the great front door, Tina accepted the proferred arm with good grace and trod down the steps beside him.

To her surprise, the Duke helped her up into a dazzlingly smart curricle and tucked a light robe over her knees. This was very acceptable, as the night had turned chilly. Without conversation, the Duke tooled his pair through the quiet night streets. It was not far from Lady Sophia's home to that of Lady Delia, and the girl hoped the silence might be maintained for the whole journey. This hope, alas, was not destined to be realized, for the big man looming at Tina's shoulder took a path through a shadowy park, and turned to face her.

"And now you may explain why you saw fit to spirit my silly niece off to see *The School for Scandal* without letting her inform any of us that you were doing so."

Unwilling to betray Flora, Tina refused to answer. There was a strained silence.

Then the Duke brought his pair to a halt. "You had better decide to explain your little stratagem, for I intend keeping you here until I know the whole."

This patronizing bullying set Tina's teeth on edge. Wanted to know the whole, did he? She turned and glared up into the dark face looming above her—too close.

"But I thought the omniscient Duke of Renfrew already knew everything—about everything," she intoned with icy sweetness.

Her antagonist threw her off again, this time by chuckling softly. "What a strange, many-faceted creature you are," he said silkily. "Pedant, coquette, schemer, enigma! Which one—if any of them—is the true *persona*? Are you shallow or wily, angelic or vicious? You will tell me now, truly, exactly why you took my niece to a play. Did you arrange for her to meet some of your less acceptable friends there? Perhaps hoping to entrap the child?"

Tina flung up her hand before he could continue. The smack of it against his cheek was loud enough to startle the high-bred team.

The Duke caught at her hand.

"That was ill advised," he said quietly.

Tina was beyond caution. "I do not have to remain in this curricle to listen to your vile insults," she flamed. "I found myself in the same box with your niece this evening, both of us having slipped away to indulge an interest which even you must admit is a natural one. I had never met Flora before, but it struck me at once that she was very young to be in such a place unchaperoned. In addition, her enthusiasm, quite natural in itself, might have been misinterpreted by a more worldly eye." She paused, trying to phrase her explanation in a way that would present Flora in a better light. She hated and despised this man, but her own feelings must not be permitted to do harm to the younger girl. She went on in a quieter voice.

"Flora was so enchanted with the whole experience that she was—" Tina sought for words—"perhaps more exuberant than—than—"

"She was making a show of herself," finished the Duke grimly. "What exactly was she doing?"

"She was—er—hanging over the railing of the box,

staring at the audience with interest and pleasure," answered Tina.

The Duke groaned. "And of course making herself the focus of attention for every lecherous—"

"She is very young," protested Tina. "She had no idea!"

The Duke drew a breath. "What next did my idiotic niece do?"

"I engaged her attention, and managed to draw her away from the front of the box. We conversed very amiably until the play started, when of course we both attended to the action upon stage. It was in the first interval—" Her voice faltered.

The Duke raised his eyebrows. "Now we get to it. You invited some friends to your box?"

"You are the most insulting, bigoted, foul-minded man I have ever had the misfortune to meet!" seethed Tina.

The Duke laughed derisively. "I know your sort! No more pseudo-virtuous bridlings, no more play-acting! I want the truth—at once!"

Tina set her teeth. "At the first interval two men came into the box without knocking. I hid in the shadows, my hood over my head. *No*, before you ask me! I had never seen either of them before. They announced to your niece that their names were Milton and Thomas, and asked Flora *who they had the pleasure of meeting*. I told them I found their grammar as offensive as their manners."

Again surprising her, the Duke laughed. "Ever the pedant!" he mocked.

"You cannot have it both ways," Tina flared. "If I am a pedant, I am not—"

"Not what?" mocked her tormentor. "You are well read enough to know that some of the greatest courtesans have been intelligent, even cultured women."

"Do you want to hear the rest of the story or not?" gritted Tina, unable to bear his mockery.

"Tell on!" His teeth flashed in a grin.

She could not understand the mood that seemed to have seized him. His eyes glinted with laughter, yet he had accused her of dreadful things! Tina shook her head, wishing that she had some of Maddy Cope's understanding of the male sex. "The proper study of mankind is man," she heard herself saying, to her horror.

The Duke grinned at her. "Now I wonder why Pope's *Essay on Man* should be on your mind at this moment? Can it be that there is a man you wish to understand?"

"Quoting poetry is a bad habit we Bluestockings have, so my Grandmother informs me. She despairs of launching me successfully. And of course she is right. With enemies like you, Your Grace, no woman could hope to be accepted in Society."

Even in the dim light, Tina could see that he was frowning angrily. "It is not my disapproval but your own immature behavior which will bar you from the Polite World! You have not yet told me what happened in the theater box tonight."

"At first," said Tina in a low voice, "the two men took me for Flora's chaperone. I had my hood up, as I told you. Flora at once disabused them—"

"She would!" muttered the Duke.

Tina paid him no attention. "They urged Flora to go down to the lobby with them for a glass of punch. I tried to dissuade her. When she insisted, I—I concocted a tale."

"Predictably," agreed the Duke provocatively.

Again the girl ignored his interruption. "I reminded her of the time her uncle discovered an unsuitable youth paying court to her. Hiring *two* bullies, this uncle had the unfortunate youth beaten into insensibility. Thomas and Milton retreated with more haste than dignity."

"Was I the rather inadequate hero of your tale?"

Tina refused to rise to this challenge. "Since I did not

then know Flora's uncle was Renfrew," she said quietly, "you were not."

"Or you would have made my role in the drama even less heroic?"

Tina continued doggedly. "After the men withdrew, Flora was alarmed at the unpleasant possibilities of her situation. We came home in a hackney. That is the story."

The Duke, silent, gave his horses the office to proceed. The journey to Tina's home was speedily accomplished. The Duke helped her out and accompanied her to the door.

"Shall I ring, or do you prefer to slip in by a side door?"

Disdaining to answer, Tina plied the knocker. Then she turned to the shadowy figure beside her. "I should be grateful if you would leave at once," she said quietly. "I shall have enough trouble without having to explain *you*."

Laughing quietly, the Duke made her a bow and strode back to his curricle. He had driven away before her grandmother's butler opened the door.

Chapter 6

*Tina's grandmother did not learn of her misad-*venture. Dolby, the butler, with whom Tina had come to be a prime favorite, simply neglected to mention that he had let Miss Tina into the house at midnight, when everyone else, including Lady Delia, believed her to be safely tucked into her bed hours earlier.

Dolby had a word with the girl as he served her breakfast the following morning. As he offered her a platter of delicious baked ham slices, the butler asked her in stern fatherly tones where she had been last night and with whom. Looking up at his kindly, concerned face, Tina told him.

His advice, quietly given and gratefully received, was that Miss Tina refrain from flouting the established rules of Society, lest she become notorious, find herself unsought, and dwindle into an ape-leader.

Much struck by this dismal picture, Tina assured him that she would follow his advice to the letter. He refilled her cup, presented the ham a second time, and expressed the opinion that the day would be fine. Tina agreed, and they parted with mutual respect.

Six days later Lady Delia came into the library, where Tina was working on her book. The girl saw at once that her grandmother was in high gig. A sympathetic smile brightened her rather solemn face.

"Do open the budget, Grandmama," she coaxed. "I can see you are cock-a-hoop about something!"

For once ignoring the child's regrettable tendency to use cant, Lady Delia thrust an invitation into her hands. Tina scanned the impressive missive with mounting interest and pleasure.

> His Grace the Duke of Renfrew
> requests the honour of the company
> of the Lady Cordelia Camden
> and Miss Athena Long
> at a Ball . . .

"But Grandmama, this is impossible—!"

"And why do you say that, you silly girl, when you hold the invitation in your hand?" Lady Delia frowned. "I wonder what caused his change of heart? I was so certain he had taken you in dislike! He is such an arrogant creature, playing Providence with everyone's life!"

"Why, then, we must refuse his invitation, and teach him that he can't direct our lives," said Tina, more cheerfully than she felt.

"Are you mad? No one refuses Renfrew!" said her grandmother absently. She was already planning her campaign to get her beloved, if difficult, grandchild firmly established in Society. "We have a week. Time to get a new dress for you, my dear. I have never felt that you looked your best in the pastels which seem to be reserved for débutantes. Pink! Baby blue! *Missish*. With your lovely, unusual coloring, I think, perhaps . . . *apricot*!"

Tina could feel laughter rising within her like a warm,

bubbling tide. The arrogant Duke had sent *her*—despised double-dealer though he had named her—an invitation to his Ball! She chuckled softly.

"*Apricot?* Are you planning to drape me in fresh fruit?"

Lady Delia rightly ignored this badinage. She went on, firmly. "Yes, that's the color! It will give your face warmth, and set off your beautiful hair and eyes. I'll go to *Melanie*. Something rather special, I think. None of this *ingénue* plainness. And the Camden pearls, of course."

Tina expressed her gratitude suitably, but there had come into her expression a little uncertainty. Lady Delia, sharp-eyed, saw it and challenged her.

"I wonder," asked Tina slowly, "*why* he has done it? Could it be some plot to pay me back for my unguarded comments at the Nairn Ball?"

"He has probably been observing your behavior at the last few functions we have attended, and has realized that your pert remarks on the evening of your first meeting were due to nervousness, and were not characteristic of you, my dear! He may be arrogant, but Renfrew is a just man, I would swear to it! I am sure that is what has happened." She stared at Tina. "*Circumspection*. That must be your watchword, Athena. If Renfrew is seen to have forgiven you, the voucher for Almack's is in our hands!"

Tina tried to master her resentment as she considered the power held by the haughty Duke. It irked her that his slightest word should determine her fate and cut up or restore her grandmother's peace. Strangely enough, she still felt that odd warm glow of happiness within her. He had changed his mind! Or, more interesting, *had a change of heart*, as Lady Delia had put it. Could it be that he had begun to like her? Tina frowned. It was probably just that he was grateful for her rescue of Flora.

Tina had not heard from the girl since the night at the

theater. She hoped her formidable Mama had not sent her into limbo as she had threatened.

Sighing, Tina watched her grandmother bustling out of the library on the first of many important errands connected with the invitation—not the least important of which would be to discover whether her old friend's granddaughter Jennifer had also been invited. Tina turned resolutely back to her composition. The book which she had coaxed Lady Delia into permitting her to work on was the fruit of an idea she had had while watching her maid and the maids of her mother and sister at Malong Hall. The young servants had been pathetically anxious to "improve themselves" so that they might be as knowledgeable as the Town servants who frequently accompanied their mistresses to visit with the Longs. At one point, Athena had decided to work with the girls, improving their pronunciation and vocabulary, as well as opening to them just a glimpse of the life of the mind.

Dulcinia Long had not approved of her bookish daughter's efforts, but she had merely warned Tina not to lead the chits to think above their station.

At which moment, in a surge of anger which quite surprised herself, Tina had resolved to create some sort of manual which young servants could use to enrich and enlarge their mental capacity. Hence the book. Of course Lady Delia had been horrified to learn what a ruinous diversion her grandchild was engaging herself in, but when, at the end of a particularly powerful lecture on the evils of appearing *bookish*, Lady Delia saw the stubborn set of Tina's soft lips, and the mulish thrust of her jaw, the older woman stopped with a despairing shake of the head.

"I can see I am not having much effect upon you, Athena! Yet you agreed to be guided by me. Do you not realize that to be known as the *author of a book* puts you at once beyond the boundaries of the Beau Monde? A literary tradesperson! It would be awkward enough if you wrote amusing verses occasionally—for such faddish dilettantism is permissable among males and safely-married females. But a book about the education of servants! I cannot think what everyone would say! Can you not at least suspend work upon this volume until you . . . that is, until—"

"Until I am safely wedded?" Tina completed wryly. "Oh, Grandmother, if you only knew how urgently I long to put my mind to use, sometimes, upon something more challenging than the latest gossip! It was the dearth of mental stimulation which drove me away from the Assemblies at home—and you knew it when you brought me to London."

Lady Delia nodded rueful agreement. "I cannot understand this need to be forever whetting your wits against a problem, but I will admit you have never deceived me about your weakness, child. Continue to work upon your tutelary tome, then, if you must," and she twinkled at the now-smiling girl, "but as you love me, *do not* let anyone outside these walls know what you are doing! I promise you, such knowledge will be fatal to all my plans for you!"

Now as she turned once more to her work, Tina wondered if, in truth, she was sensible to continue in a campaign to catch an acceptable *parti*. Acceptable to whom? Her parents wished only for their charming changeling to be happy; Grandmother had the same goal, but saw it as being brought about through marriage to a man with social position. Tina stared at her manuscript without seeing it, as she asked herself the question: What would make me happy? Then to her shocked surprise, the image of a darkly handsome, mocking, arrogant face rose before her inner vision.

. . . *Renfrew!*

The one man in all London to whom the idea of marrying Miss Athena Long would be the most repugnant! The man who had scorned, insulted, sneered at her! Who had even frustrated Lady Delia's attempts to get her a voucher to Almack's! How could his face, his name, come so powerfully into her mind? Tina put away her manuscript in its special drawer and went to her room, disturbed by her own wayward heart.

Chapter 7

Lady Delia's dressmaker produced a triumph. The apricot gown was all and more than she had hoped. Its softly rich color gave delightful warmth to the pretty face; its artful draping made the most of the small slender figure. And it was, in truth, the perfect background for Tina's lovely hair. Lady Delia caught her breath as the girl entered her grandmother's room the night of the Duke's Ball. She had never realized how huge and mysteriously golden-shining Athena's eyes could be, or how attractive was her youthful grace. The current fashion was for tall, stately blondes with massive bosoms and long-nosed, classical features. This girl was the antithesis of the mode, yet she managed to radiate a kind of magic sweetness in the new gown.

"The color suits you," announced Lady Delia simply.

Tina smiled. "I think so, too, Grandmama," she said happily. "Who would have thought a simple apricot had so much good in it!"

"Is that a *quotation*?" asked Lady Delia suspiciously. "If so, I beg you not to repeat it."

Tina's joyous ripple of laughter brought the smile back to her grandmother's face. The older woman did herself present a noteworthy appearance. She had chosen brown velvet and the Camden rubies, and offered an opulent yet modish image.

"I believe we shall do very well," she said, leading the way down to the carriage.

Her words seemed prophetic. A veritable crowd of Corinthians, Bloods, and petty noblemen surrounded Tina as soon as she had paid her respects to Lady Sophia, acting as her brother's hostess. This lady greeted her with cold civility, saying only, "Ah, yes, you are the one who is interested in Poetry," as though it were a *gaucherie*. Tina was thankful to escape to the warmth of the obvious interest of the Duke's male guests.

As for the Duke himself, she had refused to face him as she followed her grandmother down the reception line. She had kept her eyes upon his chest, tonight elegantly robed in a shirt and cravat of finest lawn. As his large hand clasped her small one, he had pressed quite hard, and turned the fingers slightly.

"What! No ink stains?" he murmured wickedly, enjoying the quick rush of tender color to the girl's cheeks.

He cannot know of the manuscript! was the girl's first terrified thought. Then she recalled that Bluestockings were supposed to be distinguished by inky fingers, or at least dusty ones, and drew a thankful breath. She moved quickly down the line, accepting introductions to the Duke's heir, Harry, who snubbed her; Flora, looking very subdued and unhappy, but brightening at sight of Tina's face; and ending with Nigel, Flora's younger brother, who had a pleasant open friendliness which soothed Tina's exacerbated spirits.

The healing continued very prosperously under the

marked attentions Tina received during the evening. In fact, the only man who did not seem to want to know her better was her host, who, after his initial greeting, did not seem aware of her presence. Tina told herself that as the host, the Duke had of course to do many duty dances, and was encouraged in this belief by catching sight of him moving gracefully around the dance floor with her grandmother. But after the elaborate and delicious supper, which Tina and Jennifer ate with four attentive young men as their partners, Tina felt a sudden weariness possess her. Somehow the evening, so eagerly awaited, had turned heavy and dull. Looking around the circle of animated faces at her table, she could not understand her deep sense of disappointment. When the group rose to return to the ballroom, Tina found herself strangely reluctant to follow.

A hard hand caught her elbow as she lagged behind.

"May I have this extra dance, Miss Long? The orchestra are playing several short dances while the guests are at dinner."

By this time, Tina and her impromptu partner were at the door of the ballroom. It was true; the musicians were rendering some dashing tunes of which a number of young couples were taking advantage. Tina recognized Jennifer and Flora, both laughing and obviously pleased with their youthful partners. Tina turned her face up to meet the Duke's intent gaze.

"This is the Children's Hour, I see," she said with a wide, lovely smile. "Thank you for indulging us."

The Duke swept her rather roughly into his embrace. "We are neither of us to be classed with the schoolroom set, Miss Long," he said, irked that she emphasized the difference in their ages.

Tina's heart fell. She had longed for this man to take

her into his arms, yet now he had done so, it seemed that they would be at odds during the brief dance. She tried another subject.

"It was good of you to ask me to your Ball," she began.

"Flora made my life miserable until I did so," the Duke replied coolly. "She has been forever plaguing me and my sister to ask you to become her companion—"

Tina stiffened in his arms.

"What arrogance!" she hissed, her small face flushed with anger. "I could have become a governess without coming to London for the Season! Do you think Lady Camden would approve of my hiring out as a servant?"

The Duke watched her furious little countenance with a rueful smile. "I have said it wrong again," he acknowledged, but Tina was too hurt and angry to listen. "I only meant—"

"You meant to put the devious little schemer in her place—as one of your sister's servants!" flamed Tina, a little restricted at having to conduct the quarrel in low tones. She tried to get out of the Duke's arms, but the maddening man merely tightened his embrace. Tina was about to create a scene when the music ended, and the laughing young couples began to move off the floor. Jennifer and her swain came up on one side, and Flora hastened toward Tina on the other.

With a sardonic grimace, the Duke made his bow and walked away. I shall go home at once, fumed Tina, but even as she thought it, she knew she could not so distress her grandmother. Making her excuses to Jennifer and Flora and their partners, she slipped away.

Not to a conservatory, she advised herself. I do not have good fortune in such a place. Opening a door, she was enchanted to discover a great library, with shelves of books on all four walls and a fine fire crackling in the grate. Tina drew a breath of satisfaction and began to prowl along the walls. Within a minute she had found a book she had often heard of but never read, and had settled herself in guilty comfort at one end of the room beside a shaded lamp.

She was interrupted in her absorbed appreciation of the book by the sound of the door suddenly being thrust open.

Facing back into the hall, a girl with a head of blonde curls and a striking green dress was speaking to someone, obviously a servant.

". . . now you will do as I instructed you—at once! Give my message to His Grace."

Tina, putting down her book reluctantly, was rising to announce her surely undesired presence when the girl went on. "Send another footman here to me this instant!"

As the girl shut the door and turned into the room, Tina found herself sinking down into the chair which was facing away from the door. The girl moved toward the fire, humming softly to herself. Tina could see her clearly in the firelight, although the great library was poorly illuminated by two small lamps. Tina recalled seeing the girl several times during the evening, for her voice was louder than average and her dress more extreme than Tina herself approved. Why had she sent for the Duke? Tina was appalled to realize that she might be interrupting a planned rendezvous, and was about to rise and make whatever awkward excuses she could dredge up, when a knock came upon the door and a servant entered.

The girl whirled to meet him. "It took you long enough," she snapped, and then went on. "Go to the card-room at once and find my father. He is Sir Oswald Pennet, a heavy-set man with a balding head. Tell him he is wanted in the Library—and stay with him to lead him here!"

Tina sank down again into the chair. There was a plan

afoot, that was obvious, but whether it would be to His Grace's benefit was not equally clear.

At this instant the door opened without preliminary warning, and the Duke strode into the room. Seeing the girl waiting for him in front of the fire, which silhouetted her figure tantalizingly, he halted and frowned at her.

"Miss Pennet! What is wrong? I received an urgent message—"

While he was speaking, Colinette walked toward him, lifted her hand to her neckline and tore her gown from one white shoulder. Then, smiling, she tousled the careful arrangement of curls on her head. Looking shockingly disheveled, she began to laugh at the expression on the Duke's face.

The door opened. With a swift movement, Colinette threw her arms around the Duke's shoulders.

A heavy-set, balding man walked into the room, observed the tableau, and roared, "Your Grace, what is the meaning of this?"

Tina came forward, clapping her hands. "Well done, Colinette! You would win a place in any theatrical company, I vow! I have never seen a better performance!"

It was hard to tell which of her three auditors was the more astounded. Then Colinette, quick off the mark, began to sob noisily. Her father stared, red-faced, from one to another. The Duke's hard, handsome countenance had assumed its wonted hauteur.

After a moment, Sir Oswald said grimly, "I demand that someone explain this disgraceful scene to my satisfaction!"

Tina smiled serenely at him. The Duke watched her intently. "I have been here in the library since supper. Your daughter came in, sent a footman to fetch the Duke, and one to bring you." She turned to the other girl.

"Colinette, perhaps you would wish to explain to your Papa what next occurred?"

Colinette hissed at her. "I wish to say nothing! The situation speaks for itself!" She cast a languishing glance at the Duke.

Sir Oswald glared at the silent nobleman who was now leaning casually against the mantel, watching the scene with an air of cynical amusement.

Sir Oswald's eyes darted from one to the other like an actor who has been given the wrong cue. Then he faced the Duke, blustering,

"How do you explain this, My Lord Duke? My daughter's disarray . . . her tears . . . ?"

"I make no effort to do so," replied Renfrew imperturbably. "I am as much in the dark as you appear to be, sir. I arrived here two minutes before you, to be greeted by this—ah—situation. I can only infer, from what Miss Long says, that your daughter has been practicing for some sort of theatrical performance, and that the two of them wished to . . . surprise us."

Sir Oswald gnawed at his full lower lip. "I cannot accept that, My Lord Duke! My daughter's clothing ripped from her—her hair falling down—"

"Why don't you ask her?" suggested the Duke, obviously bored.

The baron turned upon his daughter. "Well, Colinette, what has happened?" He glanced sourly at Tina. "What is this girl doing here?"

The blonde minx turned a furious face toward the awkward witness to her stratagem. "You were here all the time?" she blurted. "Why did you not speak up sooner? You've ruined everything, you interfering little bitch!"

Tina laughed. "Perhaps you had better mind your tongue, Colinette. Your Papa and the Duke will be guess-

ing that you had some sly little plan to entrap His
Grace—"

"That's a lie!" cried Colinette, and broke into heart-
rending sobs.

It was too late. Her father, who might have supported
her ploy had it not been for the unexpected observer, was
now as angry at his bungling offspring as he had formerly
been at her supposed seducer.

"Pull your dress together and tidy your hair," he said.
"I'll get your cape and take you home." He strode into the
hall, slamming the door behind him.

In the ensuing silence, Colinette pulled up her dress and
ran her fingers through her hair. She did not look at either
of her companions. Tina peeped at the massive, unbend-
ing figure of the Duke and glanced quickly away. He was
not frowning, but his expression, for some reason, frightened Tina.

Ye gods! she thought, with a thrill of panic, *he cannot
believe that I was party to any of this!*

Sir Oswald, grim of face, returned with his daughter's
cloak. In silence he pulled it around her.

The door was thrust open again, and a stout, sour-
visaged dame swept into the room, scanned the occupants, and said in a very loud voice, "What is the meaning
of this?"

The Duke lifted one cynical eyebrow. "Not again!"

Lady Pennet ignored him. "Colinette, why are you here
in this state of dishevelment? she began, and then her eyes
returned to her well-cloaked daughter with surprise and
censure.

"It won't fadge, Mama," said Colinette sharply. "This
—this little drab has been here the whole time."

Lady Pennet made a quick recovery. "You mean there
has been an orgy taking place in this very room?" Her

small eyes darted from one to another as she assessed her chances at some discreet extortion.

Tina gave her a complacent smirk. "I am the Duke's fiancée. Oh, we have not announced it as yet," she said, in reply to the utter incredulity on three of the four faces before her. "You will understand that arrangements must be made! I trust you will not seek to make public what you have heard here tonight? Gossip can be so awkward, can it not?" And she looked meaningly at Colinette.

Sir Oswald caught his wife's arm as she opened her mouth to continue the attack. "Shut up, Ophelia!" he advised tersely. "That cock won't fight."

When the Pennets had closed the door behind them, Tina exhaled deeply. "Phew!"

"Yes," agreed the Duke. He watched her as she walked over and sat down near the fire. "I suppose you think you have done something clever?"

"As a matter of fact, I do," admitted Tina smugly. "I believe the phrase is *saved your bacon*."

"And of course you had nothing to do with the original conspiracy," he continued smoothly.

Tina flung back her head proudly. "Your Grace, I did not!"

"I do not choose to believe you," the Duke said coldly. He held up a restraining hand. "Oh, perhaps you were not in the little minx's confidence earlier, but you were quick enough to take advantage of the situation, were you not? 'I am the Duke's fiancée,'" he quoted savagely. "And you tell me you don't know that will be all over London by tomorrow evening?"

"But I warned her not to gossip, lest I spread the story of her daughter's trick," faltered Tina.

"Are you naïve enough to think that will stop her? If she gets her story in first, anything you may say will be taken as mere desperate defence." He scanned her appalled face sardonically. "Oh, you have feathered your nest well, little opportunist!"

Tina's dark eyes met his steadily, although her face was pale. "You cannot believe that," she pleaded.

The Duke's derisive smile was his only answer.

Tina set her jaw. "I shall return home at once," she said quietly. "When I am no longer in view, any possible gossip must die for want of an object."

"Running away? Is that your only response when you have suffered a set-back?" sneered His Grace. "Think a moment! If the new fiancée suddenly disappears, what a feast that will offer to the gossip-mongers! They will be saying I have murdered you." And from the look on his face, Tina feared that was just what he would like to do.

"No, we must play the game as you have announced it, little schemer," he said coldly. "I promise you, I'll make you regret your double-dealing."

"Let us break it off, publicly," pleaded the girl.

The Duke laughed harshly. "You think that will restore my prestige? To be jilted by a wretched chit of a Bluestocking?"

"Then *you* may jilt *me*, publicly!" urged the girl, now appalled at the situation into which her light-hearted, well-meaning words had plunged them both.

His Grace regarded her consideringly. "It occurs to me that I might find a use for you, Athena. What a misnomer *that* is," he added, mockingly. "Goddess of Wisdom! You've scarce two wits to rub together, making such a totty-headed play as to claim to be my affianced wife! Why did you do it, if not to feather your own nest?"

"I was trying to save you from a rather sordid little plot which that girl was setting up under my very eyes," protested Tina.

"By seeking to victimize me yourself?" prodded the Duke scornfully. "A likely story!"

"What use—can you find for me?" pleaded Tina, seeking to end his sneering questions by harking back to his disturbing statement.

His Grace pursed well-cut lips. "It will suit me to permit the subterfuge to continue during this Season. I shall use you to fend off further attempts at forcing me to the altar."

"Are you not afraid I might take advantage of you?" challenged the girl, for some reason very sore at heart.

The Duke laughed harshly. "I am completely in control of the situation," he said. "When I am safely through the Season, I shall discover that we are not, after all, suited, and renounce the relationship. With your full agreement," he added, threateningly.

Tina glowered at him. Wild thoughts of vengeance pulsed in her mind. Renounce the engagement, would he? What if she were first to do so? In front of his friends? That would serve him right!

The Duke watched the angry, uncertain expression with an enigmatic smile.

"Go and fetch your grandmother here," he ordered. "I shall set up my strategy with her before making the—public announcement."

"Oh, cannot it wait until tomorrow?" urged Tina. Every minute she stayed close to this overpowering male, her senses weakened her will. He was so—*masculine*, all the magnificent height and strength and virility of him! She feared to draw a breath, lest his male ambience quite unnerve her.

The Duke grinned callously. "Beginning to find it is not as easy as you supposed? Get your grandmother! I won't tell you again!"

In a blaze of fury, Tina swept from the library, pursued by low, mocking laughter.

Lady Delia was more surprised than her granddaughter when the Duke announced his decision. After welcoming her to the room, inquiring after her health, asking if she had enjoyed the Ball, and receiving her gracious assurances, the wretched man cocked a derisive eyebrow at the fuming Tina.

"I have asked that you meet me here in private so that we may resolve a rather delicate situation," he began. "It has been agreed between your granddaughter and myself that we should announce our engagement tonight, at this Ball—"

The normally composed Lady Camden gasped *"What?"* and stared incredulously from His Grace to Tina. Then, making a quick recovery, she said, "But that is quite impossible! Her parents—"

"It must be tonight," said the Duke portentously.

"How he is enjoying this, the devil!" thought Tina, seeing the flow of expressions—alarm, suspicion, dismay—which moved across Delia's countenance.

"There is nothing like *that*," Tina said austerely, and was enraged to observe His Grace smothering a laugh.

"I do not understand," whispered Lady Delia. "I beg you to confide in me, dear child."

"There is nothing to confide, Grandmama," said Tina hotly, her eyes defiant upon the Duke's. "It is only that—"

"That we have agreed to announce our engagement," interposed the Duke smoothly, "and I should like it, above all things, to have you at my side as Athena and I face the guests in a few minutes." He smiled beguilingly at the confused older woman. "Will you not give us your blessing, Lady Delia? I am sure Athena's parents will be happy to be guided by your decision!"

He slanted a mocking glance at Tina. *Since you came*

here to London for the sole purpose of catching a hus-band, his smile told her. Tina had not enough *nous* to fence with a man of the Duke's sophistication. Desperately she told herself she would explain everything to her grandmother, refuse to sanction the announcement, rush from the mansion into the street—and while she was reviewing these unsatisfactory alternatives, the Duke was bowing over the hand of a suddenly gracious Lady Camden.

"Thank you for your generosity and your support," his deep voice sounded like a knell in Tina's ears. He offered an arm to both ladies, led them from the room, paused for a moment to speak a word to his imposing butler, and then led his two companions slowly and with a sudden air of great formality into the ballroom.

The musicians were resting between dances. The Duke continued his slow and imposing progress directly across the shining floor. Gradually the small party was observed, and the guests stood back to provide it free passage. It had all the dignity of a royal progress, Tina thought, unable to face the curious, envious, or startled stares of her fellow-guests.

In the event, her rosy cheeks and lowered glance did her no harm with the sticklers present. Lady Delia also contributed to the correctness and tone of the proceedings. The older woman was much liked in the *Ton*, for she was unfailingly good natured and kind. So it was with almost universal good will, albeit with rampant curiosity, that the guests crowded in after the trio to learn the reason for His Grace's behavior.

His announcement stunned his guests. There was a hiss of comment, several startled exclamations, and finally a general murmur of congratulations. Charles Vernell hastened forward, with Flora on his arm, to shake his friend's hand while Flora kissed Tina's cheek. Then the Duke indicated the doorway, where the butler appeared, attended by half a dozen footmen bearing trays of glasses.

"I invite you to pledge the health of my fiancée, and our happiness," he called out. The footmen were busy with glasses and champagne. Lady Sophia appeared at His Grace's shoulder, affronted that he had not informed her of the step he was taking, but unwilling to remain out of the limelight at this important moment. Soon the Duke had arranged an informal line of his family, Charles, Lady Delia, and Tina, to receive the guests' congratulations and good wishes.

Once or twice during the reception, after some particularly outrageous expression of his happiness in his new estate, the Duke slanted a malicious smile at Tina. She smiled back with saccharine sweetness, which unfortunately only seemed to amuse the wretched creature.

When the seemingly endless parade of well-wishers had finally passed, the Duke gave a sign to the leader of the orchestra. The musicians obligingly struck up a sentimental waltz, and His Grace the Duke of Renfrew led his new fiancée out onto the floor. Tina cast him an agonized glance.

Through a wide, fixed smile he murmured down at her, "Oh, yes, my dear, you are going to dance with me for as long as I wish. I intend to get full measure from this—this *engagement*. Now smile, and don't miss your step!"

Cruel beast! Tina set her jaw, lifted her head and swung out with all the style of which she was capable. He should not shame her in front of his curious, back-biting friends! Athena Long would prove herself equal to whatever challenge this hateful man could make.

Well content with the success of his strategy, the Duke swung his little deceiver gracefully around the floor, and a number of his acquaintances began to think that John Stone had chosen more wisely than they had at first decided. For the girl, an unknown débutante, looked positively regal—or at least, ducal—in a most attractive gown, whose warm color brought a delicately becoming flush to her pretty face. *All that lovely shining hair*, thought some of the seasoned Bucks: *how erotic it would look spread across a white pillow! And those huge, golden, eyes: how challenging they were in that sweet face! How they would melt and glow with passion!*

The female observers murmured their surprise and aired their conjectures sotto voce. It might be unwise, to say the least, to be overheard criticising the future Duchess of Renfrew. A very few dissidents openly questioned the suitability of the unequal match, and a few others demanded plaintively to be told *who* this Miss Athena Long could be, since one had never met her at Almack's! But Flora's enthusiastic pleasure in the match, and Lady Delia Camden's smiling confidence, went far to silence conjecture.

Gradually the floor filled with other dancers, and the agony of being the focus of all eyes was reduced for Tina.

"Can we stop now?" she muttered to her smiling partner.

"Do not tell me you are tiring of me already, Miss Long? I shall expect a better show of interest than that, for the duration of our engagement."

"I warn you, sir—" began Tina in a low, husky voice, "do not push me too far!"

"You *warn* me?" mocked her tormentor. "But I am sure your greedy little plan involves seducing me into making this sham engagement a reality!" He pulled her body close to his. "Does it not?"

Tina's step faltered. Wide eyes fixed upon his, her face slowly drained of color.

The Duke held her firmly, his own gaze puzzled and wary. "Are you trying to pretend that you are not the hardened coquette I judged you?" he asked. "You'll catch cold at that!"

"Your crudity offends me," whispered Tina.

"Crudity? Shall I put it in literary mode, Miss Pedant? Repeat Juliet's father's command to *fettle your fine joints*? Did you think I would accept this forced engagement without recompense?" he sneered. "I'll demand payment when I am ready. In the meantime, remember not to defy or anger me, and you will find I am not so harsh a master."

Then with a mocking smile, he returned her to the chaperonage of his sister and Lady Delia, whence Charles Vernell swept her off immediately to dance. And so it went for the rest of what was surely the most exciting Ball of the Season.

Chapter 8

The last guest had hardly disappeared through the massive front doors before Lady Sophia turned on her brother in furious confrontation. "You will explain this—this preposterous, degrading rig you are running!"

Flora and Charles, who had been laughing together at some incident that had occurred, were instantly silent as the virulence of Lady Sophia's attack registered itself upon their attention.

The Duke endured his sister's furious glare calmly.

"What rig is that, my dear Sophia?"

"This shameful, hurried announcement of your marriage, made without consultation with me—"

"What have you to say about whom or when I marry?" asked the Duke in a voice whose coldness would have warned a more sensitive woman than Lady Sophia.

"If I had been born a man!" she raged, the old, festering wound driving her to dangerous outspokenness.

"Thank God you were not," snapped her brother, for once losing his habitual composure. "For a worse representative of ducal dignity I could scarcely imagine."

Astonished by this sudden flare-up of antagonism, Charles and Flora exchanged anxious glances.

Sophia was not yet routed. "Perhaps you will condescend to enlighten me," she sneered, "just when the decision to wed this country miss was discussed with the family? I have heard nothing of it!"

"You heard it tonight, when I made the announcement."

"That does not satisfy me! To be left ignorant and embarrassed before a gaping crowd of my friends, all of whom demanded to know why they had no hint of this—this amazing development—!"

"I am afraid the satisfaction of your friends' curiosity is not a matter of moment to me," the Duke advised her frigidly.

"But you have consistently refused to consider wedding any of a number of highly acceptable young females in the last ten years!" shouted Sophia, beside herself with anger and resentment. If he did indeed intend to marry this girl, he would assuredly come up with an heir within the year—and then, alas for all her hopes!

"Perhaps I have fallen in love," suggested the Duke in the silky tones which so enraged her.

"*Love!* Pah!" she snorted. "No matter how poorly you fulfil the Ducal role, I had considered you superior to such middle-class fustian!" She paused, shocked out of her tantrum by the sudden implacable contempt on the Duke's features.

"I shall forget this entire conversation, Sophia." He stared her down until her gaze fell before his. "You would be well employed checking *Gogo's* current activities," he advised coldly. "He has borrowed against next quarter's allowance twice already, and my secretary tells me he has debts—and greedy mistresses—all over town. I will subsidize his extravagances no longer!" His voice had softened toward the end of this rebuke, but it was clear to his listeners that his decision was inflexible.

"I—I had not known," faltered Lady Sophia. "It is not a mother's business to be prying into what her grown son is doing—"

"But it *is* a sister's right to dictate her brother's behavior? To accuse him of *failing his duty* in front of witnesses?"

Sophia looked abashed as she realized exactly what she had said, but the glare she gave her brother as she swept out to her carriage was hostile and unforgiving.

"Well!" breathed Flora uncertainly. "It appears that Mama has forgotten she has a daughter."

"Charles will see you home," said the Duke absently.

"Delighted," said his friend, "and then I shall return here."

The Duke raised a quizzical eyebrow.

"As Your Grace's best man, I shall need to be familiar with all the arrangements," explained Charles with his most engaging grin.

The Duke shrugged. "I suppose it was inevitable. Well then, return if you must. I shall await you in the library."

Half an hour later, the Duke was pouring a glass of brandy for his friend. Silently he raised his own glass.

Charles was not permitting that. "May I offer my sincerest congratulations, old fellow?" he asked, his expression appropriately solemn while his eyes glinted with amusement.

The Duke looked sceptical. "Thank you," he responded. A rueful smile twisted his lips.

"It was a trifle sudden, was it not?" Charles continued. "I mean, I distinctly recall your saying that nothing on earth could get you to the altar . . . that all women could be—ah—divided into two classes—"

It seemed the Duke had not wasted his time while he waited for his friend's return. He gestured with his empty brandy glass and corrected Charles solemnly. "All women, like all Gaul, can be divided into three parts." He poured more brandy into his glass.

"Which are?" prodded Charles, grinning.

"Beautiful and stupid; bookish and ugly; and my sister Sophia. Who is, thank God, unique."

"Into which category are we to place your fiancée?" persisted the younger man.

When the Duke refused to answer, Charles went on more seriously, "Flora's *in alt* over the whole affair. She seems devoted to Miss Long. I gather they have met?"

"Yes. Athena rescued the silly little noddy when she got herself into a pickle at the theater—"

Charles frowned. "Flora was at a *theater—alone*?"

The Duke nodded. "Got some maggot in her brain and crept off by herself. Got a seat in a box which later was invaded by a couple of loose-screws, as Athena gave me the tale."

The younger man was appalled. "But John! The risk Flora took!"

The Duke frowned. "All ended well, thanks to Athena. It seems she also was eager to enjoy Sheridan's comedy, and found herself sharing Flora's box. My—ah—fiancée managed to discourage the interlopers, and brought Flora safe home."

Shocked into sobriety, Charles whistled a thankful sigh. "No wonder you are grateful to Miss Long! I take it you were able to conceal the little adventure from your sister's knowledge?"

"Happily, yes."

When it appeared that the Duke had no intention of saying more, Charles persisted rashly, "Was it from gratitude that you asked Miss Long to be your wife?" Meeting his friend's icy stare, he went on, "No, don't poker up on me, John! I know you too well. You cannot keep telling me for months on end that you despise the whole Female Sex, and then suddenly present us with a wife—!"

"I am not married yet," said the Duke grimly. "What is more, I have no intention of discussing it further. If you have had enough brandy, Vernell, I'll bid you goodnight!"

Quite unruffled by this rude dismissal, Charles laughed, clapped his old friend on the shoulder, and said, "I've often heard it said that a man becomes prey to mental disorders at the thought of entering the wedded state. I had not expected to find the imperturbable Duke of Renfrew reduced to such a pitiable state!"

"Oh, go home!" snapped the imperturbable Duke with a snarl.

After Charles had taken his leave, still laughing, the Duke sat in the library glowering over his empty brandy glass. He told himself that Miss Athena Long was a cheap opportunist, a wily schemer, and made several other disparaging judgments. Then his conscience reminded him how quickly and cleverly she had come to his defense, even after he had delivered a devastating snub and some insults whose crudity surprised himself. Why did the female get under his guard so deeply and so successfully? She had saved him when the unspeakable Pennet minx had sought to trap him. *Her* parents were probably in it, too; at least the mother was. The Duke set his noble jaw. The harridan had probably put her daughter up to it! What a disaster such a marriage as that would have been! The Pennet woman was another Sophia. At least he had Athena Long to thank for getting him out of that trap! For a grim moment he wondered how he could have extricated himself if the Long girl hadn't popped out of the shadows.

Another thought, even less pleasant, struck him. *Could* the two girls have been in an alliance to run a rig on him? It hardly seemed likely. Colinette Pennet had looked shocked and then infuriated when Athena appeared. The Duke was forced to give Athena the benefit of the doubt—at least until he could marshal some real evidence against her.

He tried again to think of another course of action which might have—how had the chit phrased it?—saved his bacon. There didn't seem to be one, except for the line Athena had taken. It had been neatly done, actually. The Duke grinned reluctantly. Little devil! She had played her role with intelligence and self-possession, letting the minx and her precious father know there had been an impartial witness to the attempted entrapment, then introducing a note of amusement that might have disarmed schemers less determined than the Pennets. Her gesture had even given them a way out, if they had wished to take it. *All a silly joke! Quickly forgotten!* A grin of reluctant admiration softened his harsh expression.

Athena. She had her wits about her, the little Wise One! At this thought, the Duke frowned again. She did indeed have her wits about her. Could a country miss, in her first Season, act with such savoir faire, such instant comprehension and mastery of the Pennet's attack? And to what—or *whose*—actual benefit? For the result of her play-acting had been to secure for herself the Catch of the Season.

The Duke's well-cut lips drew into a sneer. She had probably believed he would be grateful—or stupid—enough to let her get away with her trick! Well, John Stone would show the little plotter just what she'd won by her wiles! And make damned sure she didn't enjoy it! At the end of the Season, he'd drop her so firmly that she'd never dare to show herself in London for a second Season.

Somehow the idea of having Miss Athena Long in his power for the next few months was a surprisingly enjoyable one. Getting up from his chair, the Duke walked over to pour himself another glass of brandy. Such action had become a necessity, for John Alexander George Stone, twelfth Duke of Renfrew, now well over halfway drunk, most reluctantly found himself listening to the very small voice of his Conscience, which was firmly reminding him that his only evidence for the girl's duplicity was his own jaundiced opinion of women in general. His Conscience was also presenting him with a vivid picture of a pair of amazing golden eyes which had met his in open honesty, her very outrage at his charges disproving those same charges. In vain His Grace reminded himself that females were consummate actresses; that they were prone to duplicity; that they were at the same time wily and stupid. And quite incapable of loyalty to anyone or anything but themselves.

It was no use. He could not get those lovely eyes, so open and honest, out of his memory. In a quite uncharacteristic act of fury, the Duke flung his brandy glass against the fireplace and smashed it into pieces. *All right!* Athena Long was not a schemer! The Duke prided himself upon being a pretty acute judge of his fellow men—and women—and to the best of his knowledge and belief, Athena Long was neither dishonest nor self-seeking.

And so he would still continue to enforce the control he had gained over her. He would use her as a shield against the scheming little Pennet and her ilk. And at the end of the Season, he would give Athena a rare treat (at the moment unspecified), and perhaps even assist her toward that suitable match for which she had undoubtedly come to London.

The thought pleased him so little that the Duke, completely exasperated, staggered upstairs to his ducal bedchamber in a fury all the blacker for being incomprehensible.

Drunk as a wheelbarrow! judged the footman, putting out the hall lights thankfully. He did not blame his master. Any man, caught at last, was entitled to drown his sorrows.

Driving home in her luxurious town carriage, Lady Delia beamed at her surprising grandchild. It would seem that, in spite of several severe handicaps, the child had, virtually unaided, captured the finest Prize in the Marriage Stakes.

"Are you going to tell me how you did it?" she demanded, when she could wait no longer.

Tina showed no disposition to be coy. "I was trying to save him from a scheming female—and he let me," she said morosely.

Naturally Lady Delia could not rest until she had discovered the whole story. Then, sitting back against the squabs, she began to chuckle. "I might be tempted to comment that 'Fools rush in—' except that no one who has pulled off the *coup* of the Season could be labelled a fool. How do you and your fiancé intend to proceed?"

Tina's sore heart misgave her. The Duke's scarcely veiled threats, his crude insinuations, had left her with no desire to prolong their association. Surely he had not meant what he implied? He had been angry, of course. He had rightly resented the manipulations of the Pennet girl and her parents. But surely he had seen her own action for what it was? An impulsive, perhaps foolish, but never self-seeking gesture to defend an innocent man from being blatantly victimized? She sighed.

"Let us wait and see what His Grace wishes to do," she begged. "I am sure he will have a fine plan to get us all out of this entanglement. You know, even better than I, how absurd it is to think of him wishing to wed me!"

Lady Delia was smiling. "We must burn your manuscript at once," she decided, in a characteristic non sequitur. "Do not mention your book, I beg of you! It would be more than enough to wreck everything if it were even hinted that you—write." The last word was a whisper.

Some unconquerable spirit within the girl caused her to admit with a wry smile, "But dear Grandmama, I took the finished book in to the printer today. Perhaps that is our way out of this intolerable impasse! He can shed me without shame to either of us!"

"Do you really think so?" inquired her grandparent. "The Duke may find some on the fringes of society who would not condemn him for breaking his plighted word, but you, poor child, would be best advised to enter a nunnery at once—or go back to Malong Hall," as though the two alternatives were equal in ignominy.

This matter-of-fact judgment was sufficient to stifle dialogue. The two ladies rode on in silence.

Chapter 9

Lady Sophia Rate arose at an unseasonably early hour the next morning, determined to discover the full and true facts in the matter of her brother's engagement. For all that she was arrogant, mean spirited, malicious and vindictive, she was not stupid, and nothing about last night's announcement was in her brother's usual style. Throughout a wakeful night she had searched her memory for any detail, however small, about the unworthy Miss Athena Long. Lady Sophia spent the morning following up these scanty clues. By noon, she rested in triumph.

After a refreshing nuncheon, she sent a footman with an urgent invitation to Miss Long in Portman Square, and summoned Flora to her sitting room.

The girl arrived happily, bursting into excited comment upon Uncle John's engagement.

"I would rather hear a little more about the poetry-reading you attended with Miss Long," said her Mama, repressively.

Flora's eyes widened apprehensively, and she lost some of her bright color.

Her mother nodded sourly. "There was no invitation to a *soirée*, was there? Or if there was, you did not accept it. Do not bother to lie about it! I have talked to Lady Gracelle Manning. She informs me neither you nor Miss Long attended her poetry-reading."

"You are determined to have it all over London," accused Flora. "Have you no care for my reputation?"

"That is what you are here to talk about," snapped Lady Sophia. "Where exactly did you go that evening, and how does that Long girl come into it?"

Haltingly, with frequent corrosive comments from her Mama, Flora told her story. When she was finished, Lady Sophia said, "At least, between you, you have kept the matter from becoming common knowledge—one thing to be thankful for in this imbroglio! I shall send you down to Bodiam Castle today, and then see what is to be done about rescuing Renfrew from this harpy's clutches. She has used your folly for her own selfish gain."

"Miss Athena Long," announced the butler, issuing the girl into Milady's sitting room.

"Be seated," commanded Lady Sophia. Then, meeting Tina's cool glance, she said, less harshly, "If you please."

Tina, smiling gently at Flora, took a chair close to her.

"You may go to your room, Flora," said her mother.

Flora drew a sustaining breath. "I would prefer to remain," she said. "It is my future, you know! And I don't wish you to say things to Athena which will hurt her . . ." Her voice trailed off under the impact of Lady Sophia's astounded stare.

"You are defying me, Flora?"

"You so often say—things which—which I'm sure you don't mean. I would not have you tell Miss Long I did not love her as dearly as a sister," said the girl doggedly.

"Just what *did* you wish to say to me, Lady Sophia?"

asked Tina, to divert her hostess from a further attack upon the younger girl.

"I wished to inform you that I know the whole of the disgraceful romp you led my daughter into at the theater—"

"Mama!" protested Flora.

"Be silent, or I will have you taken to your room! I wished to inform you, Miss Long, that your little game is ended. Whatever the threats you have used to prevail upon Renfrew to make you an offer, they will not avail you now. I intend to denounce publicly the whole conspiracy. I give you this single chance to break off the engagement at once. Tomorrow I shall act!"

"You have no hesitation at blackening your daughter's name, or making your brother a laughing-stock?" asked Tina coolly.

Her poise surprised her antagonist. Lady Sophia continued in a lower voice. "Renfrew may have to suffer a few jests, but our position is strong enough to weather the storm of conjecture and criticism," she said complacently.

"You hate him, do you not?" asked Tina. "I had heard it said, but had not believed it. Your own brother! And do not forget that his consequence is, in part, your own. The name will suffer if you do as you say."

"I shall of course make it worth your while to renounce Renfrew," her ladyship continued, paying no attention to what Tina had said. "I have notified my secretary that a lump sum is to be brought to me here in a few minutes. You will take that and leave London. *After* having renounced your claim to my brother publicly."

Flora began to cry softly. The girl's grief was the last straw to a sensibility already exacerbated by the insults, unwarranted assumptions, and general nastiness of Lady Sophia.

"I seriously hope you have not, in fact, given your

secretary such an order, Lady Sophia," Tina said in a low, tightly controlled voice. "I intend going to His Grace immediately to inform him of your threats. I am sure he will be able to deal with your plan as it deserves."

She walked out of the room, down the wide stairway, across the ornately furnished hall and out through the front door to where her grandmother's carriage waited in the street. Seated within its comfortable interior, she gave way to the shock and dismay which had shaken her at the disclosure of Lady Sophia's venom. It was several minutes before she could steady her voice enough to give directions to the waiting groom.

"Please ask Tom Coachman to take me to the residence of the Duke of Renfrew," she managed.

When the carriage was rolling on its way, Tina sank back against the velvet squabs and dealt with the tempest of alarm, fear, and mounting anger within her. Through it all persisted a picture of poor Flora, frightened and crying bitterly, her red hair bright above her pallid little face.

When the coach drew up before the Duke's Town House, Tina was ready for the encounter. She was able, with a steady glance from her amber-brown eyes, to intimidate Cullon, His Grace's butler, into leading her to the library. Within minutes, the door swung open again, and a grim-looking nobleman advanced toward her.

"If you say, 'To what do I owe the honor of this call?' in that odiously toplofty voice, I shall strike you!" she told the big man.

A smile slowly softened his harsh expression, but it did not have a similar effect upon Tina's temper. "Do not laugh at me!" she snapped. "Thanks to your impossible sister, we face social disaster!"

Silently the Duke indicated a comfortable chair. Tina sank into it, being by this time ready for support of any kind. He took his place close to her.

"Try to calm yourself, Miss Long."

This reasonable request acted like a red cloak to a bull.

"*Calm* myself—? Just wait until you hear—"

"I *am* waiting," said the Duke unforgivably.

Without further ado, Tina emptied the budget. As she spoke, His Grace's countenance assumed a grimmer aspect. At the end he rose sharply to his feet and began to stride up and down.

"How long ago did Sophia spew out this detestable nonsense?"

"I came directly to you from her house."

"We shall return there at once."

"*You* may go there," objected Tina. "*I* shall certainly not do so. If I am forced to listen to any more of her venom, I shall—do her an injury!"

His Grace glanced at her sharply. "What *do* you intend doing?"

"I am returning home to Malong Hall today. I wish nothing more to do with any member of your family."

"Not even poor little Flora?" asked the Duke softly, taking what Tina felt was a despicable advantage of her softheartedness. Then, before she could respond to that appeal, he said with a cold smile, "So we see exactly how much your protests on her behalf are worth! Run away to your rustic retreat like a scared little mouse, then, Miss Bluestocking! Or is it that your pedant's heart is too dry and self-absorbed to admit a lonely child?"

Quite justly enraged by these unwarranted and diverse attacks, Tina clenched her small fists and glared into her tormentor's icy countenance. "Of course I care about Flora! Did I not miss the Sheridan play to see her safely home? But I can scarcely admit her to my heart if she's banished to a remote castle somewhere—probably locked in a dungeon!" She halted, glowering at his suddenly sympathetic face. His warmth affected her like the sunshine breaking through clouds. She drew a trembling breath, her eyes wide on the handsome face so close to her.

The disturbing creature seemed well aware of the effect he was having upon her. "You are quite a little fury, for a dry female pedant, are you not? I had not known that soft amber eyes could flash with so much fire!" Tina found herself disarmed as he continued in a civil tone, "If I can promise that Flora will not be sent down to moulder in the dungeons at Bodiam, will you in turn agree to remain in London and befriend the child? That was all I meant when I asked you last evening to become her companion, you know. Just be her friend, and accompany her to all those delightful places she hungers to see—Astley's Theater, the Wild Animal Enclosure, Mr. Sheridan's latest play." He paused, and his fine grey eyes ran over her changing countenance with a wicked sparkle. "Of course I shall have to accompany you both to that particular diversion, shall I not? Perhaps with Charles? He too has a fondness for little Flora."

When Tina, too startled by this change of manner to reply, continued to stare warily at him, the Duke smiled and went on, in a strangely offhand way, "Of course there would be a few other—ah—obligations."

Tina would not permit herself to be duped by this new, wily softness. "Exactly what other obligations?" she demanded.

The Duke shrugged. "Since you yourself announced our engagement in the presence of one of London's chief gossips, who had no reason to think kindly of either of us at that moment, I imagine you might be aware of your obligations. Unless," he went on with some of his normal provocativeness, "you really *were* trying to trap me yourself?"

Much though she resented it, Tina was forced to admit

the logic of his comment. "I have *told* you I only did it to save you from being trapped by that Colinette! I could not permit *anyone* to be so ensnared!" she protested. Unwisely, as it proved.

For His Grace retorted reasonably, "If that is true, you must remain in London to give credence to our mock-engagement, must you not? We shall have to be seen together at a few important *soirées*, perhaps at some balls, and certainly at Lady Sally Jersey's Ridotto, a highlight of the Season—and your entrée to Almack's."

Tina was stunned. The bitter, unapproachable nobleman was acting as though he actually found the idea of squiring Miss Athena Long to fashionable entertainments to be a pleasing one! More amazing, he had somehow secured an invitation for her to the Season's most important function, and, if his last remark could be credited, a voucher for her to attend the most exclusive club in London. Tina stared at the dark, saturnine corsair's face, which was regarding her with complacent arrogance. *What was he up to?* Was he showing her these delights, only to snatch them from her outstretched hands? Tina had no way of knowing. So, being Tina, she asked him.

"Why are you doing this for me, when you already had me barred from Almack's?"

"Perhaps I regret my hasty action. We are supposed to be engaged, you know."

Tina addressed her attention to that aspect of their problem almost with relief. "You will need to harness your sister's malice pretty promptly, if you wish our pseudo-engagement to be received with credence in the *Ton*. She warns me that if I am not out of town by tomorrow morning, she will spread the story that I took Flora to the theater and introduced her to some questionable persons in order to force you to propose marriage."

"Is Sophia aware of Colinette's attempt to blackmail me into an engagement?" asked the Duke sharply.

"I said nothing about it," answered Tina, "and no one else except the Pennets know. They would hardly be eager to spread the news of their daughter's trick, surely?"

The Duke frowned. "It is impossible to judge how far Sophia would go in her efforts to embarrass me," he said at length. "I believe we must confront her together, at once, and try to stop her vicious tongue. Come, Athena!"

Rather to her surprise, for she would have wagered a large sum that *nothing* would get her into That Woman's house again, Tina found herself being ushered into Lady Sophia's presence shortly thereafter.

Their hostess greeted them with a predatory smile.

"Now I wonder what can bring such an unlikely pair to my drawing room?" she sneered. "Can it be my threat to make a certain announcement?"

Watching the Duke's face, Tina wondered with a small frisson of alarm how even his redoubtable sister dared to use the word *threat* to him. However, when he spoke, the Duke's voice was level and unemotional. "No, Sophia, I came to return your compliment."

Her confidence shaken, Lady Sophia demanded that he explain himself.

"You did me the courtesy of warning me that you were going to spread a canard about my affianced wife and your own daughter. You know it is a lie—Flora and Athena have told you so. Yet, knowing it will dishonor our ancient and honorable name, make it a target for scorn, you still persist in your threat?"

"I have courage, John," Sophia blustered.

"Then I will now give you notice of *my* intentions. A warning, if you like." There was not even a hint of softness, of mercy or pity, in the Duke's iron glance. "Tomorrow morning I shall instruct my agents to refuse to pay a single bill from George's creditors. The large amounts they currently give him, for his mistresses and hangers-on, at his urgent pleading, will no longer be available. Further, George is, from tomorrow morning, to be persona non grata in any residence or club of mine . . ."

Lady Sophia presented a face livid with scornful anger. "Is this supposed to bring me to my knees?" she snapped. "It will do George no harm—"

"You had best consult with your son as to that, Madam," said the Duke coldly. "The exclusion applies also to yourself. You are no longer welcome in any house of Renfrew." His lips curled in a thin, mirthless smile at the sudden look of dismay that crossed her face. "If we Stones are to give our private affairs to the *Ton* for discussion, let us give them something worth chewing upon!"

Lady Sophia looked as though her brother had struck her in the face. Shock, disbelief, fear were clearly visible in her expression. "You jest!" she managed, through lips suddenly slack.

"You think so?" asked the Duke softly, in such a tone that even Tina, a noncombatant, felt afraid. "Ask yourself how well your proposed treacherous debasing of our name matches your constant claim that you should have been the Duke. There have been men—and women, too—of our line who would have suffered torture rather than permit what you so lightly threaten! Perhaps you should retire to Bodiam to think upon your responsibilities to our family."

Silenced, Sophia stared at him, her face ugly with warring emotions.

"Give George my message," said the Duke, and led a silent Tina from the house.

The girl remained silent as the Duke handed her into his town carriage. When they were once more rolling through the streets, the man glanced at her, his expression forbidding.

"No comments? No frantic questions, no female flutterings? Have I reduced you to terrified silence?"

Tina faced him calmly. "I am sure you are now about to inform me as to my part in your plan," she said.

One dark eyebrow quirked derisively at the girl's self-possession. "You continue to surprise me," he said, in a milder tone. "Is it time for me to determine which of the roles you play is the true Athena Long? Or is there anything to you but a set of masks?" He threw one arm lightly across her shoulders and drew her toward him with irresistible pressure.

After a single frozen instant, Tina allowed him to pull her against his chest. She kept her glance fixed on his face, her expression wary but without fear. He held her so, against his chest, for a long moment, his gaze intent. Then, still without words or tenderness, he bent his dark head and pressed his lips against hers with passionless force.

Tina had never been kissed by a man outside her family before this moment. She found the experience astonishing. First she was aware that his skin had a fresh smell from some aromatic soap or perhaps a masculine lotion. His hard embrace made her aware also of the scent of fresh linen, and an interesting warm tang that probably came from his flesh. She took a delicate sniff, to confirm her theory.

The Duke's heavy-lidded eyes opened wide and focused on the lovely, small face so close to his. But Athena had already moved on to a second surprise in this business of kissing. His lips over hers tasted of some kind of flavor, which was a blend of aromatic and bitter. It was vaguely familiar. Surely her father and brothers often carried just that piquancy on their mouths?

"Beer!" she announced happily, drawing her face back from his relaxing hold in order to speak. "You have been drinking beer!"

The Duke's stern face melted into a rueful grin. "It is usually considered a restorative after too heavy an indulgence in liquor the previous evening," he admitted. Tina, looking into his eyes, was conscious of a strange new feeling deep inside her, so powerful that it shook her. It also showed in her small, exquisite face. The Duke's arms tightened around her again.

"You are a very odd little siren," he said huskily. "First sniffing, and then—tasting!"

"It is my first real kiss, you see," she explained carefully. At his elevated eyebrows, she added, "Of course I do not count my father or Killy or Jase!"

"And who are Killy and Jase?" demanded the Duke.

"My brothers," explained Tina. "And you must not think they are all forever kissing me, for they are not! It is only upon birthdays, or Christmas, or when they have returned from a trip—or had an especially good day with the Hunt."

"Legitimate occasions for celebration, surely," admitted His Grace, feeling suddenly very much in charity with his world. He had a virgin! Better, he had a girl who could amuse and even surprise him, jaded worldling that he was! He settled the fragrant little armful more comfortably into his embrace, and then, with the practiced gallantry for which he was well known in some circles, he bent his dark head once more to Tina's lips and kissed her, this time with seductive sweetness.

When he lifted his head, Tina shivered involuntarily. Her golden eyes were wide with startled awareness. After a moment, she moved out of his arms and sat back in her corner of his carriage.

The Duke also sat back. "You do not subscribe to the

conventional modes of behavior, Miss Long?" he asked finally.

"If you are asking me why I am not babbling, weeping, or—or bridling, My Lord Duke, I can only say that I am not your conventional débutante."

The Duke uttered a harsh bark of laughter. "An undeniable truth." He too had had an enlightening experience, but he was by nature and by training better equipped to conceal his emotions. He reached out and took her hand, not gently, not even flirtatiously, but with a hard demonstration of his power to control. "Exactly *why* did you come to London?"

"I came to find a husband," said Tina baldly, her eyes on his.

The Duke crushed her hand in his large fist until an involuntary gasp of pain passed her lips. Then he flung the hand from him as though it were repugnant to his touch.

There was another heavy silence, which lasted until the coach drew up in front of Lady Delia's town house. The Duke regarded Tina coldly. "I shall require you to remain in London for the next few weeks. You will hold yourself ready to accompany me to whatever social gatherings I decide to attend. My secretary will send you a list. I shall expect you to be ready when I call for you, to present a good appearance, and to behave with propriety and whatever charm you can summon up—"

"Is this elaborate charade necessary?" asked Tina in a low voice.

"It will be expected of the —ah—newly-engaged couple," the Duke said on a sneer.

"And if I do not agree to it?"

The Duke's groom had come to stand outside the still-closed door of the coach. The Duke himself bent forward to scan Tina's expression. "Are you telling me you will not do as I suggest?"

Rather than giving a direct answer, the girl repeated, " 'Suggest'? Say rather *command*! You know you do not expect disobedience. What of my own life?"

The Duke drew an exasperated breath. "Do I need to remind you, Miss Long, that it was your—*inspiration* which orginally established our engagement? It cannot harm a husband-seeker to appear to have snared the finest prospect in the matrimonial stakes."

"Are you saying that a man of integrity will be willing to accept a woman you have publicly rejected?"

"You are now trying to convince me you have scruples?" The Duke shook his head, and tapped lightly on the window. His groom at once opened the door, let down the steps, and offered his arm. The Duke got out, assisted Tina down and walked beside her to her grandmother's door. "My secretary will be in touch with you. Stay in town," he said softly, and returned to his carriage.

As he drove away, John Stone found himself feeling, for the first time in his adult life, rather at a loss. It angered him to realize that the occasion for his uncertainty was a green girl, totally without Town bronze or sophistication, but with a mind, he dared guess, as sharp as a man's. A girl who savored his person and tasted his lips with the innocent freedom of a child, yet who held grimly to it that her sole purpose in coming to London was to snare a husband. His lip curled with contempt—and then he remembered the innocent sweetness of her lips, and the wide, clear gaze of her magnificent eyes. A paradox! How could any one female be at once conniving and honest; sensual and innocent, maddening, infuriating, and . . . desirable?

Deliberately he relaxed his powerful shoulders against the squabs. There were important matters to be dealt with, not the least of which was the attack of Sophia Rate. Had the woman finally lost her wits? Her threat required a visit to his man-at-law. And then, he thought with relief, there was the matter of the new pamphlet he had been advised of. What good fortune if the very material he needed was ready to his hand! The schools he had been painstakingly establishing, one on each of his country estates, had desperate need of teaching materials. Four good instructors he did have in hand, newly down from Oxford or Cambridge, not yet fully decided upon a life's work. It had been the devil of a chore seeking out the four young men, far more trouble than convincing his tenants and the village people that their children would benefit beyond their wildest reckoning if suitably instructed. The professional men and the great landowners sent their offspring to good schools, many of which required that the child be registered at birth in order to secure a place. They had no need for his *country schools*. But the background level of education was very low for the rest of the populace: bright children had literally no place to go to learn to better themselves.

It was not that the Duke wished to make his tenants discontented with their lot. Rather, he wished to give them means to improve it, and get greater satisfaction from it. So he had conceived the idea that brainpower was as precious a resource as good fertile fields and healthy animals, and had, in his usual arrogant fashion, set about to establish training centers. The tenants were conditioned by hundreds of years to accept their overlord's ideas as not only valid but irrevocable. The young scholars he had found with some help from Charles Vernell, allowed into the secret. But the books, the training manuals, were another matter. He did not want goody-books, the part fairy tale, part nursery-rhyme handbooks. Nor could he use, with these quite unlettered children, the volumes and texts used by college students.

During one of his desperate searches among the publishing houses of London, he was delighted to discover that a very clear yet simple basic handbook was under preparation. The Duke was not put off by the information that the book was primarily intended as a training manual by which young servants could improve the skills that would enable them to better their own positions. The proofs, when he saw them, were, to his astonishment, interesting, bright, and so attractively presented that even the dullest mind might find them persuasive. He studied the proofs more carefully. They revealed a remarkable familiarity with literature, both ancient and modern, with several languages—including the classic Greek and Latin—and with mathematics and even rudimentary science.

A treasure!

The Duke's interest was further aroused when, upon demanding to know the name of the author of this excellent brochure, he was told that the author wished to remain anonymous.

"Some noted scholar pressed for a little spare cash?" he suggested lightly to Mr. Thomas Sinclair, the junior partner in the publishing firm of Guthrie and Sinclair.

Mr. Sinclair looked unhappy. Although the Duke's curiosity was now rampant, he decided to drop the question in favor of the more urgent business of securing a great many copies of the useful work.

"How many shall you wish, Your Grace?" asked the hopeful Thomas.

"Begin with one hundred, but keep the plates or whatever it is you print them from. I may need more very soon."

The gratified publisher, mentally rubbing his hands, thought to interject a word for future reference. "The—er—author of the book might be persuaded to do others, more advanced, more challenging to the juvenile intellect," he offered craftily.

The Duke nodded. "Well, we shall see. When the first of these is ready, send a copy around to my house by hand, at once, if you please. Then I shall be able to judge of its usefulness. A sturdy cover, of course—resistant to ink and chalk!—and within, paper of good quality, with bright illustrations. The whole must appear attractive. Of course, *no mention of my involvement is to be made.*"

"Yes, Your Grace!" Sinclair was bowing. "As per our contract."

There was a silence and he looked up to meet the quizzical gaze of a pair of very knowing grey eyes. "When am I to be informed of the name of our author?"

"I gave my word, sir," stammered Sinclair. "As did my partner, Mr. Guthrie. It is a matter of—"

"Honor?" the Duke had suggested, faintly smiling.

Sinclair barked a laugh. "A matter of contract," he had admitted. "The author would not sign unless we promised to conceal—the identity." With this, the Duke had had to be content.

It seemed to His Grace a most striking coincidence that when he came into the hallway of his Town House after depositing Athena at her grandmother's home, he should be presented with a heavily wrapped parcel from Guthrie and Sinclair. He had been thinking of them, and the treasure they had found him, all the way home. Well, not quite all the way. He admitted that he had turned to thoughts of his secret project to rid his mind of very uncomfortable visions of a slender girl with silky black hair and amazing golden eyes. Opening the parcel eagerly in his library, he sighed shortly as he admitted further that it was not the girl whose memory disconcerted him, but the harshness of the contempt with which he had taken his leave of Miss Athena Long.

And then all thoughts of her or any other problem were driven temporarily out of his mind, as he scanned the students' handbook, called *The Roads to Wonder*. And on the bright orange cover, etched with magic lines, was a great city, pure and clean and towering in its majesty, a focus and an enchantment.

The Duke stared at the cover of his new teaching manual for a long time.

Chapter 10

❧

The first person besides the butler whom Tina encountered in the spacious entrance hall was her grandmother's dresser. Hugget had apparently been waiting anxiously for her arrival, and conducted her at once to Lady Delia's sitting room.

The older woman greeted Tina eagerly. "What did that hag Sophia Rate want of you?"

By the time Tina had finished her report of events at the Rate Town House, Lady Delia was very angry indeed. "I cannot believe that even Sophia Rate would so perilously endanger her own family's reputation," she fumed. "Did the Duke tell you what he plans to do?"

Tina presented a censored version of His Grace's orders. "We are to hold ourselves ready to attend any functions to which Renfrew decides to accept an invitation." She hesitated. "Or perhaps his command was only for me. I am not sure."

Lady Delia frowned. "But our own invitations? Are we to refuse them, unless they coincide with Stone's?"

"The Duke's secretary will bring me His Grace's choices

every morning," Tina explained woodenly. Then her eyes darkened with emotion, and she said, huskily, "Is this how matters are managed in ducal households, Grandmama? I see I have much to learn."

Lady Delia rose almost without thinking, and enveloped the forlorn girl in comforting arms. She was aware that there was something very wrong about the situation, but her first thought was to restore the lovely laughter to her beloved grandchild's face. She said wistfully, "When you recounted this bizarre tale to me last night, I felt sure that behind the rather melodramatic trappings of the engagement there was a sturdy core of genuine liking on both sides." As the girl began to object, Lady Delia spoke again. "No, do not try to argue with me! I know enough of His Grace's force of character to believe he would never permit himself to be cozened into a declaration he found utterly distasteful!"

"He could have made no defense against the situation in which, thanks to Miss Pennet's manoeuvrings, he found himself," stated Tina. "What excuse could he have given the affronted parents of Colinette when they discovered her in his arms, with her garments disheveled?"

"But you told me that you had announced that you had been there from the beginning! You are not one of the Patronesses of Almack's, exactly, but you did guarantee chaperonage of a sort," snapped Lady Delia.

After a charged silence, Tina faced her grandmother bravely. "I begin to believe you are in the right of it. His Grace might have braved it through, given the protection of my presence, had I not thought it necessary for him to have the further shield of a prior engagement. To me." She sighed. "So you see he has good foundations for his suspicion of me. I spoke too impulsively, but he might well believe that I spoke—with well-planned strategy!"

"You babbled romantic nonsense, like the bookworm

you are!" corrected Lady Delia crossly. "It is not to be wondered at that the Duke is out of patience with you! Have you any real objections to marrying the man?"

Tina flung up her head. "The insuperable one: that he does not wish for the connection! He is convinced I am a scheming, unprincipled creature—and he fully intends to . . . to dispose of me at the end of the Season!"

Her grandmother raised thin eyebrows. "He told you this? Or have you concocted another—*story*? By what means does the Duke of Renfrew intend to *dispose* of his fiancée at the end of the Season? In an oubliette?"

To Tina's horror, a sob escaped her. She swallowed and then firmed her lips. "We are to announce that the engagement is ended—by mutual agreement," she managed. A tear rolled down her pale cheek.

Her grandmother considered this news. After a moment she said, in a quiet voice, "There is only one thing to do, Athena. You must follow His Grace's lead, do just as he asks you, and present a pleasant and dignified front to the *Ton*. Your own credit, and your family's, depends as much as Renfrew's does upon your good sense and stability."

"Yes, Grandmama," said Tina, who had never felt less sensible or less stable in her life.

The first order of business, decreed Lady Delia, was for Tina to go with all haste to Guthrie and Sinclair and request the return of her manuscript.

Fortified by a cup of tea and a change into her prettiest redingote, the girl proceeded to the publishers that very afternoon. She went on foot from the corner, having ordered the coachman to pick her up at that exact spot in exactly half an hour—these being the only terms upon which he would agree to drop her off. As she approached the pleasant but quite undistinguished building which housed the activities of Guthrie and Sinclair, she was horrified to observe a tall, handsome figure striding in her direction.

"Miss Long?" said the Duke, on a rising note. "Whatever are you doing in this very commercial area of the city?"

Tina's wits, though shaken, did not fail her. She cast a lightning glance around her, and observed two hanging boards which proclaimed the nature of the business being carried on within the buildings. One said: CANES, CRUTCHES, INVALID'S CHAIRS. The other proclaimed, under the rather daunting representation of a glaring eyeball, SPECTACLES, QUIZZING-GLASSES, LENSES. Tina smiled.

"I am getting myself fitted for a pair of spectacles," she offered.

For the barest instant, surprise and regret showed on the Duke's face, and then his eyes narrowed and his expression became unreadable.

"Indeed? I commiserate with you. A pity to have to cover so unusually beautiful a pair of eyes."

Tina found herself blushing under the obvious admiration of the huge man. Forcing herself to smile up into his dark face, she went on, "I am not really too concerned, Your Grace. I shall need them only for reading."

"I should say, reluctantly, that you may be more in need of them than you believe," the disturbing man objected. "Since you are on the wrong side of the street and going in the wrong direction to achieve your goal." The creature had the bad taste to laugh!

Tina's delicate pink blush became the rose of anger. She cast a hurried glance across the street and verified his charge. Then she opened her mouth to verbalize another falsehood, but her noble opponent beat her to the post.

"Now do not tell me that Lady Delia is in need of a Bath chair, or a crutch! I shall not believe you, and I shall at once report your canard to the lady herself!" He grinned down at the angry girl, obviously enjoying her frustration. "Now tell me, without deceit or roundaboutation, what brings you to this neighborhood?"

Tina's small chin was lifted. "But I told you, Your Grace! I am going to order a pair of spectacles! Perhaps you will be good enough to give me your arm to the shop? Lest I fall over some obstacle," she added for good measure.

The Duke offered a strong arm cased in elegant superfine. "On one condition," he said softly. "That you stop calling me Your Grace. We are plighted, are we not? Therefore it is quite *convenable* for you to call me by my name."

"Stone?" teased the girl, her beautiful eyes sparkling. It was such a joy to talk to this man when he was in this smiling, playful mood. She did not want it to change, ever. If only—!

But he had placed his hand over hers on his arm, and was pressing it firmly. "Not my family name, witch! My own!"

His fingers were long and slender considering their strength. Tina dimpled up at him. "Alexander?" she asked. "Surely nothing less than the name of the conqueror of the world will do!"

The Duke stopped her as they were about to cross the street. His hand held hers very tightly against his other arm.

"Athena! You invite the lightning!"

The lovely face was a delight in its demure sweetness.

"*Kaliespera*, Zeus!"

The Duke's eyebrows shot up. "One might believe you were as Grecian as your name! Bidding me *good-afternoon* in the classic tongue. You name me greatest of the Gods? I wonder what you have in mind?"

Tina shrugged, a little disconcerted. "Harmless play, with one who has the background to share it with me," she said, her eyes not meeting his.

The man cursed himself for the suspicion that had shattered the joyous exchange. He moved ahead to the goal he had had in mind. "You are to call me John," he instructed her.

Tina nodded.

"Now," he persisted, feeling awkward, and decades older than the quiet girl at his side.

"Yes, John." The words were little more than a whisper.

The Duke squared his shoulders. His cynical attitude, forever seeing connivance and intrigue in the simplest action, had destroyed a moment of pure joy. John Stone, who hadn't indulged in Tina's sort of "harmless play" within his own memory, did not know how to recoup that which he sensed he had lost. And so, moved to anger by his loss, he acted the part of the man he had become.

"Where is your carriage?" he said sharply. "What is Lady Camden thinking of, to permit you to wander unescorted through the streets?"

"Tom Coachman is returning for me within a few minutes. We did not think I could come to harm on this quiet street!" she protested.

"Lady Delia knew you were coming here?"

"Of course! I am not so rag-mannered as to—" then, meeting his quizzical glance, she blushed again. "The clandestine trip to the theater was the only time I have ever gone out without her full knowledge and consent!"

The big man stood staring grimly down at the girl. "Tell me the truth, Athena! Did you come to be fitted for spectacles?"

The wide golden eyes met his honestly.

"I did not. But I beg you will not ask me why I came, for I cannot—*must* not—tell you! I can only assure you that there is nothing—wicked, or hurtful to any person, or *shameful* in my visit."

The piercing grey eyes met hers with an intentness which seemed to seek the very secrets of her mind and heart. After a long moment, the Duke released her hand and turned to survey the street.

"We shall wait here for your carriage," he said.

Tina did not want to stand beside this man who showed so clearly that he did not trust her. She could feel unhappiness rising like a tide within her. She glanced up to study the harsh handsome profile of her companion. As she did, a sort of courage began to stiffen her drooping shoulders. Why should she feel guilt, whose only crime was to prepare a manual to help servants to better their condition? Her chin rose in what her brothers would have recognized as a fighting stance.

"I think I will tell you my reason for coming to this street," she announced. "Since it seems so important to you—"

The Duke's head turned sharply toward her. His eyes were hostile. Then his gaze went beyond her shoulder to a carriage which was almost racing down the quiet street.

"That is *my* carriage!" he exclaimed, and lifted his hand to arrest the coachman's progress.

When the vehicle had drawn to a swaying halt in front of them, the Duke demanded, "What the devil is going on, Wilson?"

It's Miss Flora, sir," gasped the coachman. "Cullon's just had a visit from Sir Charles Vernell. It seems Miss Flora has disappeared, and Lady Sophia is shouting that you're hiding her somewhere. Cullon sent me to find you."

The Duke wasted no time. Hoisting a reluctant Tina into the coach ahead of him, he detailed the groom on the box to stay behind and explain to Lady Delia's driver where Miss Long had gone.

Tina leaned across him to call out the window, "At the corner! Todd was to meet me at that corner!" While she was still gesticulating, the carriage lurched into motion, and she was thrown backward into the Duke's arms. He received her upon his chest with no signs of discomfort, but she said crossly, "This is poorly managed! It were better for me to wait for Todd on the corner. This way, my grandmother will be beside herself with anxiety! The most *bungled* situation!" She glared up at the man who was still holding her closely. He was *smiling*!

Tina's brows drew down into a horrendous frown. "How did your coachman know where to find you?"

John chuckled unforgivably. "Took you long enough to get to that one, didn't it? I had informed Cullon, of course, before I left the house, that I was going to walk down to Fort Street to get—" he paused and closed his mouth slowly. He was not smiling.

Tina was on his hesitation like a flash. " 'To get'—what? And don't tell me *you* need either spectacles or a crutch!"

"I cannot tell you," said the Duke blankly, and then his lips twisted into a wry smile. "Do you suppose we might try confiding in one another, Athena?" he said, more gently than she had yet heard him speak. It seemed that the need to trust disturbed and confused him.

The girl drew a slow, deep breath. There was nothing she could do to change what John Stone's life had been up until now, nor to influence the character which that life had molded. But perhaps, if they shared new experiences, she might be able to convince her cynical, disillusioned Duke to trust her—possibly even some day to like her. It was a hope worth nourishing, Tina decided. At this moment the carriage drew up before Lady Sophia's mansion.

Charles Vernell was awaiting its arrival in the street,

and ran over to open the carriage door at once. He helped Tina out, and even spared her a smile, but immediately afterward his anxious gaze was fixed on John Stone's face.

"She isn't with you, then? I had hoped—" he stammered.

"Inside, Charles," said the Duke firmly, and swept them both along with him into the drawing room.

There Lady Sophia sat, her face a twisted mask of anger and fear. "What have you done with them? What trick is this, Stone? What do you hope to gain by interfering in my affairs?" She was speaking shrilly, her eyes glaring at her brother. "Is this a ploy to discredit me with the *Ton*?" She noticed Tina, standing at Renfrew's shoulder, and her voice rose to a shout. "This scheming little upstart! What is she doing in my house? Has she something to do with my children's disappearance? I'll wager *she's* at the root of it!"

"Calm yourself!" snapped the Duke. "You rant like a Bedlamite!" He continued in an icy tone, "Is it true that Flora is missing? Control your hysteria at once, if you please! I wish to hear facts, not unbridled screeching!"

But Sophia, glaring from John to Tina, refused to speak. It was Charles Vernell, mastering his alarm and concern, who informed his friend that Flora had left the house three hours earlier, and had not returned. She had also, it appeared, taken a small satchel with her, containing some clothes. She had not left any message.

Lady Sophia got to her feet and advanced upon the group in the middle of the room. Her eyes were bulging with rage.

"You will tell me at once what this means! What plot you are hatching to discredit me!"

A quiet voice, youthful but hard, spoke from the doorway. "You yourself have driven her away from us, Mama," said Nigel, entering the room and closing the great doors behind him. "Your endless berating and complaints, your utter lack of real interest or tenderness—!" His voice broke over the last word.

"What do you know about this?" John asked. "Tell me at once!"

"When I returned from riding this morning, the first person I encountered in the hall was Groat, who informed me that Flora had asked him to summon a hackney for her. He tried to discover where she intended to go, but she refused to tell him. Then she borrowed two shillings from him for the fare."

The Duke's rigid mouth softened a fraction. "Not a distant goal, then."

Nigel was looking accusingly at his mother.

"Groat reports that Flora was crying. He held the door open for her when the hackney arrived, and heard her give your address, Uncle John. I remounted at once and rode to your Town House. Cullon was more forthcoming than Groat had been. It seems that Flora, being threatened with banishment to Bodiam and then to a girls' boarding school, had decided to seek sanctuary with Uncle John. Feeling," added Nigel with dark challenge, "that since he had promised to give us the treats of London, he would at least protest Flora's being removed before she had tasted even one!"

The Duke acknowledged the shrewdness of Nigel's blow. "*Mea culpa,*" he said quietly. "I *had* promised Flora treats, and fully intend to give them to her, with a charming companion." He glanced at Tina. "But there has not been time—"

"Time to be banished to outer darkness," persisted Nigel.

"Is she there, then, in my house?" The Duke kept to the issue at hand. "Cullon gives her refreshment?"

"No," reported Nigel grimly, "Flora appears to have been in a panic at not finding you at home, Uncle John. She set out again in her hackney, having first borrowed a further ten shillings from Cullen."

Again, almost against his will, the Duke smiled. "We are to suppose Flora contemplated a longer journey this time," he murmured.

"How can you jest about this, Stone?" demanded Lady Sophia.

"Better to laugh than weep," said John Stone, to Tina's surprise. He looked at her, catching her curious glance. "Let me guess where Flora was bound. She directed the driver to Lady Camden's house?"

"But that's exactly right!" breathed Nigel respectfully. "Cullon managed to overhear her directions."

"But of course, failing to find me, she would go to one who had been her loyal champion upon a previous occasion—"

"She is there—in my grandmother's home?" asked Tina eagerly, a smile of relief upon her face.

"No," replied Nigel gloomily. "When she found you also away from home, she refused the offer of tea which your grandmother made her, and insisted that she had an important meeting—elsewhere."

"But what is this?" demanded the Duke. "Where is the little ninnyhammer off to?"

Lady Sophia seemed to have lost interest. "When she becomes tired of her childish naughtiness, she will come back—and go down to Bodiam, as I told her she must. Her trunks are packed."

Looking at that adamant countenance, Tina knew it would be useless to urge or protest. Lady Sophia was enjoying the idea of punishing her daughter for wilful disobedience, and demonstrating to Flora's well-wishers that they were powerless to aid the girl.

The Duke did not seem to understand that he was defeated.

"And if she does not return?" he suggested mildly.

Lady Sophia glared at him. "What do you mean?"

"I merely state the obvious. Your daughter has been gone for several hours. We know she had inadequate funds. *Where is she?*" Then, when no one answered, the Duke continued, "Is she wandering on foot through the streets? For we know no self-respecting cabman would carry her about *on tick!* Or has she decided to join the company of actors and actresses in whom she was interested enough less than a week ago to run off to—without notice to any of us?"

Lady Sophia's face bcame congested. It was plain from her harassed expression that she could not immediately find an answer, nor, more importantly, anyone to blame for this latest disaster.

Tina said slowly, "I do not think Flora would go again to the theater. Her first experience there frightened her."

"If you know so much about my daughter, Miss, can you tell us where she has gone?" sneered Lady Sophia.

"Perhaps to one of her other friends?" suggested Tina.

"She has none. She is invited nowhere. Nor would I countenance it. She must not go about socially until she has her come-out!"

The Duke regarded her with loathing. "You have had your young daughter in London for several months and made no push to bring her into the company of other girls? But this is folly! How do you hope to fire her off if she knows no one? To say nothing of the loneliness and boredom to which you have condemned her. I cannot believe it even of *you*, Sophia!"

Tina had been wracking her brain to discover a clue to Flora's whereabouts. Suddenly a picture surfaced in her mind: the supper extra-dances at the Duke's ball . . . Flora's glowing little face under the bright red curls as she whirled about the floor with her youthful gallant. And dancing nearby was . . . Jennifer Nairn!

Tina turned to the Duke. "Flora may be at the Nairns'," she said quietly. "They seemed very *easy* together at your ball. And if the poor child knows so few other girls—"

The Duke took her arm. "We'll go at once," he told Charles and Lady Sophia. And then, grimly, "I believe I must insist that you permit Flora to remain in London for the Season, Sophia. I shall stand the nonsense for her clothing and activities."

Although she would have died on the rack rather than admitted it, Sophia Rate was thankful to have so easy a solution to her problem. Renfrew would find Flora and bring her back. But better, he would assume financial responsibility for the chit, and even take her about under his aegis. And perhaps he would relent in his harsh judgment against poor George, who had been screaming at his doting Mama ever since he learned what her attack upon his uncle had brought upon him. Sophia began to smile. She had helped her older son, and without having to apologize to John or to that little provincial he was sponsoring! A good day's work! She looked about her to see who remained in her drawing room. It was empty. Charles had left with John and the girl, apparently. Sophia pulled the bell to summon a servant. It was time to write a triumphant message to poor George.

Chapter 11

Charles insisted, rather cavalierly, upon being included in the search party. After a moment's consideration, Tina interrupted the Duke's efforts to dismiss his friend.

"We do not wish to seem like gaolers hauling off a prisoner. I think Flora would find it more comfortable to be picked up by a group of good friends, dropping by for a social call."

Charles and Nigel were impressed by her suggestion. The Duke agreed, but asked wryly, "Will that work if Flora's told the Nairns her whole story?"

Tina said confidently, "We shall rely upon your *nous*, John, to carry off the situation, in that case."

Charles and Nigel grinned openly. The Duke was understood to remark upon the fate likely to befall scapegraces and would-be jokesters who pushed their Elders and Betters too far.

"*Elders*, certainly," pronounced Charles, greatly daring.

As a result of similar badinage, the Duke's party

arrived in high gig at Nairn Town House. The Dowager Duchess was delighted to welcome John Stone, for whom she had a soft spot, while both Flora and Jennifer seized upon Tina with cries of pleasure. Tina noticed, also, that Flora turned a pretty shade of pink under Charles Vernell's obvious relief and happiness in seeing her safe. So it was an unexpectedly jolly little party that sat down for tea in the handsome drawing room—so different in every way from Sophia Rate's cold and cheerless salon.

"We have been planning some interesting excursions," said Tina, striking while the iron was hot. She glanced quickly under her lashes at the Duke, who appeared willing enough. "Oh, all very educational, of course," she hastened to assure the Dowager. "Art galleries, and museums, and perhaps a concert! We were hoping you might permit Jennifer to make one of our little group."

Smiling fondly at her granddaughter's imploring face, the Dowager gave cheerful permission. "If you, my dear Renfrew, are to be their guide and mentor . . . ?"

With a rueful grin, silently acknowledging her strategy as well as Tina's, the Duke said he supposed he would have to do so, lest Flora be sent rusticate to her aunt's country home at Bodiam. Then, observing Flora's blushes and the Dowager's conscious expression, the Duke was confirmed in his suspicion that his scamp of a niece had opened her budget.

This was confirmed when Jessica Nairn asked, "Why does Sophia Rate threaten to send Flora to Bodiam Castle? Isn't that Lady Stone's home?"

"Lucy sensibly refuses to live there," replied the Duke. "The place is falling down, and so steeped in history that it has a crowded feeling. It is also cold and damp. Lucy rarely goes there since Theo died. And of course Sophia believes she has a right, as Theo's sister, to send her children there if she wishes. There is always staff in residence. The fourth Duke acquired the castle when he married the Earl of Bodiam's only child—a red-haired daughter." He ruffled Flora's hair lightly, smiling at the girl. "As copper-tops, you and Nigel have the best right of any of the Renfrews to be there."

"I would far rather stay in London and see the sights with you and Miss Long!" said Flora. "You did promise—?"

"Yes! I promised," agreed the Duke. "Now we must make our plans for tomorrow. Shall we visit the art collection of Sir Hans Sloane in the British Museum?"

"How about topping that off with a visit to Astley's Amphitheater?" suggested Nigel, hopefully.

"And then going back to John's Town House for a snack and some practice in dancing?" coaxed Charles, his enthusiasm making him appear as youthful as Nigel. "The ballroom is being wasted!"

The Dowager and the Duke exchanged glances.

"I commiserate with Your Grace," said Lady Jessica. "I foresee a crowded calendar."

The next few weeks were the happiest in Flora's life. Aside from the fact that her imposing uncle arranged exciting expeditions almost every other day—"to give us all time to recover from our excesses in between!"—Flora had the felicity of Charles Vernell's laughing escort. Tina was aware of the girl's feelings, and was finally sufficiently troubled to request a private interview with the Duke.

He received her in his library, a most impressive and fascinating apartment to such a bookworm as Athena Long. Her fingers itched to ruffle among the pages; she was hard put to maintain her image of the light-minded débutante.

It seemed His Grace was amused by her dilemma. "When we are alone, Athena, you may surely set aside that frivolous manner and indulge in your secret vice? If I promise never to breathe to a soul that the charming and popular Miss Long is, in fact, a Bluestocking?"

She was unable to prevent herself from smiling into his dark, teasing face. He was such a disturbing man—one minute warm and playful, the next—and for no reason, it sometimes seemed—harsh and cold and arrogant. Still, he was playful at this moment, and Tina wished to bask in the warmth of his good humor.

"You tempt me almost beyond bearing," she dimpled up at him. "With such treasure as you boast here, I really cannot understand how you find time to lead the Social World as you do."

"I lead until I am bored," he admitted without false modesty. "Then I disappear for a week or so—and the tongues wag!" His laugh was cynical and quite uncaring.

Chilled by his change of mood, Tina looked soberly up into the handsome countenance. "It is about Flora that I wish to speak to you," she said slowly. "She is a darling, but still very young, very unsophisticated. I am afraid she may be developing a *tendre* for Lord Charles."

The Duke frowned. "What evidence have you?"

"Oh, there is nothing *out of the way* in the behavior of either Flora or Lord Charles, at least that I have observed. It is only that Flora is still a child, and Charles is very attractive to a lonely girl."

"If my dear sister had made the least push to secure young companions for her children, we should not be facing such awkward situations," said the Duke grimly. "Nigel is to go back to school soon, and is perfectly happy with the necessity, but his departure will leave Flora the more bereft."

"Jennifer Nairn is a good friend to her," offered Tina. "And *I* care very much for the child. She will not be completely alone."

The Duke eyed her gloomily. "She will have her come-out next year. It was to put her in the way of Society that I invited her to my ball. I have seen what happens when a green girl is thrust into the *Ton* without preparation!" He shrugged. "I suppose I might arrange for her to go to a girls' school. At least she would not lack for suitable companionship there."

"Since she has not thus far attended such an establishment, and will have few of the skills expected of a girl her age, she will be put with girls much younger. Might this not seem to her a punishment?" asked Tina anxiously.

The Duke frowned. "Sophia's failure to take responsibility creates painful situations. But she is heartless!" He shrugged. "I thank you for your warning, Athena. I'll look into the possibilities of girls' schools. Meanwhile, let us continue with our policy of—ah—educational expeditions. I'll keep my eye on Charles and see what he's up to." His faintly amused, abstracted air implied, to Tina, dismissal.

She slipped away quietly. *It's as well he didn't try to stop me*, she told herself as she returned to Lady Delia's house. *I must get down to Guthrie and Sinclair and find out what has developed with my training manual.*

There seemed to be a conspiracy against Tina in this latter decision. First Lady Delia insisted upon knowing where she had been. The respect Tina had for her grandmother's kindness and social skills urged the girl to confide the problem of Flora and Charles. Lady Delia did not seem overly concerned.

"Charles Vernell is a fine young man who will prove a steadying influence on Flora as she matures. There isn't an ounce of vice in him, Tina! I knew his parents well, and from what I have seen of him—and it's been a good deal this last two weeks!—I am not at all worried as to his motives or his behavior."

Tina sighed. "With that recommendation, *Grandmère*, I can put aside my alarms and get back to serious business!"

Her grandmother peered at her suspiciously. "I do not think I like the sound of that remark, Athena," she said repressively. "Exactly what is this 'serious business' you wish to get back to?"

"Why, discovering the fate of my manual, of course!" replied Tina with a lightness she did not actually feel.

Her grandmother's frown justified her apprehension.

"I understood you had withdrawn that—that incriminating document weeks ago, Athena. Do you tell me you permitted it to be *published*?"

"I fear so, Grandmama," admitted Tina.

"Under your own name?" demanded Lady Delia.

Tina shook her head slowly. "No. Although I must admit that I regret my cowardice. After all, it is fairly scholarly, quite sound pedagogically, and—I think—even interesting." She faced her grandmother's horrified frown bravely.

"'Pedagog . . .'! Great Heavens, Tina! What is *in* the book?"

"You know," answered Tina stubbornly. "I explained it most carefully to you the last time you asked."

"I cannot have been listening," mourned her agitated relative. "You are sure your name appears nowhere in the text? And that the publishers have *sworn* not to reveal it?"

Tina's color was rising. "Grandmama, it is not a lewd or vicious pamphlet! I cannot agree I should be ashamed of it!"

Her grandmother was not appeased. "It is pedantic, bookish—and absolutely fatal to your success in the Beau Monde! I told you—!"

"But I am already engaged," retorted Tina angrily, "or had you forgotten? My career in the Beau Monde has been crowned by my successful entrapment of its greatest Prize, the Duke of Renfrew!" She ended on a short, anguished sob and turned away.

At once Lady Delia moved to take the girl in her arms.

"There, there, child! Do not weep, I beg of you! It is quite ruinous to the complexion." She patted Tina's shoulder gently until the ragged sobs ceased.

Tina raised her head and turned the full battery of amber-gold eyes upon her worried grandmother, who thought, as she had so often done recently, that the Duke must be a singularly cool and stolid male to be impervious to the bright, sensitive beauty of this charming young woman. Or was he? She had accompanied the little group to a performance of *The School for Scandal*, in the role of chaperone, and had had plenty of opportunity of observing the Duke's attitude toward his pseudo-fiancée. It had seemed to Lady Delia's expert eye that the nobleman was not as detached and uncaring as he pretended to be. *However!* This was not the time for Tina to be playing off her tricks. If indeed the Duke was beginning to feel an interest, or even an attraction, toward Tina, the fragile structure must not be jeopardized by such boring and ridiculous starts as publishing a training manual for servants! Lady Delia shuddered with real apprehension.

It was with her reluctant consent, therefore, that Tina set out in the smaller (and less noticeable) carriage, with only Tom Coachman as escort, to finish up her business with Guthrie and Sinclair of Fort Street.

As the footman was assisting her into the carriage, Tina caught Tom Coachman's eye. She was sure there was an urgency present in that small dark orb, a sort of unspoken request for dialogue. It was, however, quite ineligible to hang in the door-aperture of the carriage and shout at him, so Tina got inside and permitted the footman to close the door after her. During the ride to Fort Street, there was of course no opportunity for speech, and when the carriage drew up at the corner, a safe distance from the unimposing entrance to the premises, Tina had to get herself out of the vehicle and close the door after her. She looked up at the coachman.

He seemed anxious to communicate some sort of warning or advice, and Tina thought she understood his concern. He was either alarmed at the possibility of her being recognized in his unfashionable district without a chaperone, or he was anxious that she return to the corner within the assigned time limit. Giving him her lovely smile, Tina said quietly, "Don't be worried, Tom! I shall meet you here in exactly twenty minutes, as Lady Camden ordered."

Old Tom Todd did not appear satisfied. He leaned toward her as she stood on the narrow stone footpath. "I'll be awatchin' for ye, Miss. Stay within the doorway, if ye please! I sh'll drive right up to ye, and ye must *nip in*! This ain't a good neighborhood!"

Nodding her thanks for his special care, Tina trod happily along the footpath to the premises of Guthrie and Sinclair, Printers and Booksellers.

Chapter 12

☙❧

Tina was almost running as she approached within a few feet of the entrance to Guthrie and Sinclair. The reason for this unseemly haste was not eagerness to collect whatever monies the publishers might have for her. It was, instead, because a natty curricle bearing two obvious Bloods was approaching her at a dangerous clip along Fort Street, both occupants of which had caught sight of her and were making their interest very plain. They were either under the influence of liquor or were the rudest creatures she had yet encountered in London. Feeling like a rabbit running to earth, Tina scuttled into the shop with her head bent, unwilling to risk a second look at the rowdy pair, lest she had met them at one of the social functions she had recently attended.

As she closed the door safely behind her, Tina beheld Mr. Sinclair approaching, his face one wide smile. It struck her that she had never encountered a Mr. Guthrie. Was he perchance a recluse, or merely a figment of Mr. Sinclair's imagination?

Chiding herself for such levity, she accepted Mr. Sinclair's greeting and attended to what he was saying.

". . . happy about your book! The purchaser has given us an initial order for one hundred copies, with a possibility of a further sale!"

He waited for her delighted praise of his salesmanship, but Tina was more interested in the unknown purchaser. "Do you think that someone here in London is actually planning to open a school for servants! What a generous and far-seeing person! A rare philanthropist!"

Mr. Sinclair was privately of the opinion that the Duke of Renfrew was far from fitting the flattering image the girl was creating. Having had to cope with His Grace's keen wits while making the financial arrangements for the printing and sale of the books, Mr. Sinclair thought that *philanthropist* was the very last title he would bestow upon the wily and knowledgeable peer. Up to every rig in Town, was the Duke of Renfrew!

"I am constrained not to divulge the Purchaser's plans for your book, Miss Long, but I may say it is not to be used in London."

"Not?" echoed Tina, surprised.

"More importantly," continued Mr. Sinclair, "the Purchaser wishes to be informed if the Author is capable of preparing a further manual or manuals of increasing difficulty and—ah—challenge for the student?"

"But of course!" breathed Tina, thrilled at the prospect of stretching her mind in such an interesting project. "When would I need to have it ready?"

Mr. Sinclair awarded such naïveté a pitying smile. "As soon as possible, Miss Long." He ventured a small pleasantry. "Yesterday?"

The young lady gratified him with a charming gurgle of laughter. Rather reluctantly, he got to business and had her sign the contract for one new manual every six months until both Purchaser and Author were content to end the agreement. The money did not seem as important to the Author as did the details of the difficulty of challenge and scholarly development. This, divulged Mr. Sinclair, might present awkwardness, as the Purchaser was adamant about maintaining his anonymity.

Tina frowned. "He seems an odd person," she said discontentedly. "How can I shape and grade the work if I have no idea of his requirements?" She assessed the publisher's expression. "Can you explain to him that a clearer picture of his special needs would materially expedite the actual work of preparation?"

Mr. Sinclair bowed. "I can try, Miss Long." He sighed at the prospect of trying to pin down the arrogant peer. "There is, as you know, one plan which would resolve all difficulties."

At her doubtful glance, he elaborated, but without much hope. "If you and the Purchaser were to confer together, all problems could speedily be resolved, and plans satisfactory to both Author and Purchaser could be formulated."

"Impossible!" said Tina firmly. "Please ask the Purchaser to sketch his needs briefly. Then you can mail me the material."

With this lengthy and not too satisfactory method of dealing with the problem Mr. Sinclair was compelled to be content. He handed over a surprising number of golden guineas to the gratified Author, and ushered her politely out to her waiting carriage. Tina rode home to Lady Camden's Town House in a glow, planning further manuals in which she might entice the servants into an exploration of some of the more easily understood sciences and humane studies.

A rude reception was awaiting her.

A worried Dolby ushered her at once into Lady Delia's private sitting room, where a tall, arrogant figure stood stiffly in front of a window while his hostess surveyed him with poorly concealed alarm.

"Flora!" guessed the Author, her gaze fixed upon the Duke's forbidding countenance. "Something has happened to her . . . ?"

For once in her life, Lady Delia felt herself inadequate to control the situation. "No, not Flora, dear child—*you!* His Grace has been given some news which—that is, I am sure it is the merest tattle-mongering—idle bibble-babble—" She faltered into silence under a fierce glare from His Grace's outraged eyes.

Tina endeavored to pull herself together in the face of this unexpected disaster. Of course someone had told him about the manual! But was that any excuse for such histrionics? Surely being affianced to a Bluestocking was not enough to put even so high a stickler as the Duke into a passion? Perhaps it was the fact that she had not informed him of her literary efforts, thus arming him against surprise?

Then, lashed by that ice-cold glare, she felt a defensive anger begin to rise within herself. *What business was it of his?* They both knew their engagement was a fraud, maintained in order to protect His Grace from the attentions of over-eager females! Still, no one but themselves and possibly Lady Delia knew it for a hoax. Trying to be fair, Tina accepted that to expose so haughty a peer to the malicious amusement of his associates was disastrous.

These thoughts ran through the girl's head in a lightning instant. Now she walked slowly toward the rigid figure and said, softly, "It is not so bad, surely? If my being a Bluestocking embarrasses you so deeply, perhaps it might give you the opportunity you wish for breaking off the engagement?"

Two things happened immediately after Tina's speech.

Lady Delia groaned incoherently.

The Duke stepped forward and seized Tina's shoulders in fingers of iron, shook her till her head jerked about dizzyingly, and gritted between set teeth, "Bluestocking? Is that what you call your activities at the *Venus Club*?"

Tina put her hands on the Duke's arms and tried, unsuccessfully, to stop his shaking her. "Milord!" she gasped, "If you kill me, you will land yourself in a worse imbroglio than whatever you are in at the—the Venus Club!"

"I," said the Duke in an arctic voice, "have never entered the portals of the Venus Club! I leave that to such rakehelly rounders and libertines as Cazyion and Pitchell. Who informed me, not half an hour since at White's, that they had observed my wife-to-be entering those same portals. On Fort Street," he added in tones of deepest censure. "Where I myself encountered you recently, and was given some tarradiddle about spectacles and Bath chairs!"

Tina's delightful laughter rang out, to the shocked surprise of both her companions. "You do not tell me," she asked primly, "that *you* were on patrol that day anywhere near the profane establishment? For such I must take it to be, considering its name and the contempt in your voice?"

Lady Delia moaned again at such daring provocation. The Duke's gaze had hardened, and the icy hauteur of his expression was flaming into anger.

Tina took advantage of the momentary shock to continue her reckless teasing. "Since you seem willing to accept as truth the unsupported lies of 'rakehelly libertines,' perhaps I had better correct your misapprehensions. I was in Fort Street that other day and today in order to finish the sale of a training manual which I have been writing this past six months. My destination on both occasions was—the premises of Guthrie and Sinclair, Publishers."

She smiled coaxingly at the flabbergasted Lady Delia. "Do not be unhappy for me, Grandmother! It was bound to come out! And you know as well as I do that my engagement to His Grace was not ever a *real* one! No doubt he will be relieved to terminate such a contaminating alliance at once, the risks inherent in his *great desirability* in the Marriage Mart being so much less than those of associating with a lady of licentious habits—such as writing manuals for the self-improvement of servants!"

The Duke's expression had now become imperturbable. There was still a very angry glint to his eyes, and a tight-held line to his lips, but of the furious disgust he had shown, no trace was left.

"So you claim to have sold a book, do you?" he asked. "Who was the—ah—purchaser?" His hooded glance studied her face intently.

"That I am not at liberty to reveal," Tina said bravely. "I can, however, show you a copy of the work, which I have brought with me from today's meeting." Then with a flash of spirit, she concluded, "Such a connoisseur of the Rites of Venus as The Most Noble the Duke of Renfrew will have no difficulty in discerning the difference between a celebration of those rites and a manual for improving the speech of servants!"

Lady Delia's response to this pert provocation was a mournful squawk. His Grace was of sterner stuff. Even the glint of anger in his eyes faded, and his expression, as he stared steadily at the girl, was impenetrable. Tina had a sudden frightening awareness of her fate in the Beau Monde when the lying story circulated: a frozen rejection which would deny her very existence. Her face whitened.

"Just so," said the Duke smoothly. His eyes had never left her face, correctly interpreting her change of expression. "It seems the Author must confess her crime or risk being sent to Coventry on far more disastrous charges."

"But surely—can *you* not silence their lies?" pleaded Tina.

"The thought of challenging both the contemptible creatures had entered my mind, only to be dismissed."

"Dismissed?" echoed Tina forlornly.

"Such a challenge to a duel would serve only to spread the tale, and convince everyone that there was truth in the canard," explained the Duke condescendingly.

"Then I shall leave for Malong Hall today, leaving Your Grace free to repudiate me however you wish," said Tina, not daring to glance at her grandmother's devastated countenance.

Even this sacrifice did not appear to propitiate her inquisitor. Shaking his head slowly, he said, "You disappoint me, Athena. I had not thought so determined a campaigner for marital bliss would be discouraged by a simple set-back! Running off home like a whipped—ah—bitch!" He turned to the wide-eyed Lady Camden. "You must forgive my seeming coarseness of phrase, Lady Delia! I merely sought to use a cant phrase correctly—in the presence of a Bluestocking!"

Tina closed her mouth on a small gasp. *The devil was enjoying this!* Determining to leave the consideration of why his mood had changed so remarkably in the last few minutes to a later time, she took up the challenge of his last remark with kindling blood.

"In offering to return to my home, I sought only to reduce the embarrassment which my grandmother would naturally feel at this *quite* unwarranted, vicious attack upon my reputation by two of Your Grace's cronies—"

The maddening man held up a restraining hand. "*Not* my cronies, I beg of you!" he uttered in a quelling tone. "I could not permit persons of such bad *ton* to claim even a nodding acquaintance with me!"

Tina stared, and even Lady Delia was regarding the nobleman with a suspicious frown.

"What are we to make of this new start?" she challenged.

His Grace elevated his fine eyebrows. "Why, that I intend to make the best of this predicament, Lady Delia." His expression and tone hardened. "We shall proceed as though no vile charges had been made. Next Friday, we are pledged to attend Lady Jersey's Ridotto, are we not?"

"Your secretary brought us your orders this morning," said Tina resentfully. "Together with the box containing my costume."

The Duke nodded. "Since I am doing myself the honor of escorting you both," he said with what Tina considered to be intolerable smugness, "I naturally wished to be sure that our costumes would not clash."

"After the charges those men made at White's Club," Tina found her own anger rising as the Duke's seemed to cool, "it might be wiser for me to attend as a nun, or an abbess."

"Quite ineligible!" countered his Grace. "In these circumstances, *never* an abbess! You are, Athena, too much the ingénue to know it, but that is a very naughty term borrowed to designate a—lady engaged in venery." His hard eyes glinted mockingly.

Reassured by His Grace's good humor, Lady Delia tittered and cast an archly reproving glance at him. Tina shook with anger at his lack of sensitivity. "And what is this costume you have chosen as suitable for me?" she snapped.

"You tell me you didn't look at it?" mocked the Duke.

"I haven't had time!"

"A very pretty costume in the Grecian mode," contributed Lady Delia, who *had* looked. "After the Elgin Marbles, I should say. White and gold, my dear, with a charming golden cup with two handles for you to carry. Awkward to dance with, however. But no matter!"

Tina drew a deep, steadying breath. Grecian? That meant a clnging drapery, one shoulder bared . . . it did not appeal to the disgruntled girl as a costume in which she would wish to present herself to the Duke's friends. "A golden cup?" she repeated nastily. "Are we to go as the Nobleman and the Barmaid?"

The Duke, who had spent some time in research, was justifiably annoyed at this display of malice. "In deference to your claims of scholarship, I had planned for us to represent Hebe and Heracles."

"Hebe," said Tina, pleased in spite of her ill-humor. "The cupbearer of the Immortals! But Heracles? You would say it is a Labor to escort me?"

"Her husband," supplied the Duke coldly. "Who said she had the power of making him young again."

"But how charming!" cooed Lady Delia, who was of the opinion that few if any of the other guests would have either knowledge of or interest in mythological characters, in spite of the fuss being made over those broken statues from the Parthenon which Lord Elgin had secured for the British public! Still, it was a pretty thought, and Lady Delia hoped her difficult grandchild would accept it as the gracious compliment it probably was.

Tina was indeed wrestling with her emotions. On the one hand, such a thoughtful and unusual idea surely indicated a concern to please a young woman whose tastes were known to be classical. On the other hand, such a pair of costumes might make their wearers a laughing-stock in the *Haut Ton*. Consider Lady Sophia's reactions, or Lady Lucy Stone's—neither one known for the depth or breadth of her formal education! She raised her eyes to encounter a sharp scrutiny from the Duke.

"Well, Athena?"

Tina chuckled. "I am wondering, Your Grace, what *your* costume looks like? Is it draped to expose a manly torso? We must remember that the climate in Greece is considerably warmer than that of England in winter!"

"Draped or undraped," retorted the Duke coolly, "Heracles will escort you to the Ridotto on Friday night!"

As he took his leave and went out into the hallway, Lady Delia's lips quirked into a forgiving smile. "He is arrogant and autocratic and domineering—but he is such an *attractive* man!"

"It is to be hoped," said Tina glumly, "that he will not look absurd in his costume in front of all his friends!" She sighed. "Or that I will! I had better go up and see what he has chosen for me to wear."

Chapter 13

The next day began very badly.

Tina was still in the breakfast parlor when Dolby ushered in a weeping Flora. The older girl rose, offered tea, cocoa, coffee; Flora refused all comfort.

Taking the girl's hand in hers, Tina led her to a chair and sat down beside her. "Now you must tell me what is upsetting you, dear Flora, for I cannot help you until you do so."

Flora sobbed once more, then pulled out a wet little handkerchief and scrubbed childishly at her face.

"It is Mama!" she announced, and began to cry again.

"What has she done?" Tina persisted. "Flora, tell me!" Though she had rather take the unhappy victim in her arms, Tina gave her a gentle shake.

This firm treatment had the desired result. Flora took a ragged breath and was understood to say that her mother, jealous of the time and attention which Renfrew was lavishing upon Tina, Flora, and Nigel, had informed Flora that unless Gogo was included as one of the party, Flora and her brother must refuse all future invitations.

Tina had heard, from various sources, a good deal about Gogo, none of which would lead her to suspect that that amateur rakehell would be caught dead in most of the places the small party visited. Being Tina, she said so at once.

"Your brother would dislike our little excursions intensely."

"I know that!" Flora wailed. "You know it! Uncle John does! Even Gogo knows it, but Mama *does not*! Or perhaps she wants to make trouble for Uncle John. She hates him, you know, because he is the Duke, although she is older! She will ruin everything! I hate her!"

Tina, startled by the intensity of the feeling in the girl's voice, could find no way to deny her charges.

Flora was going on, this time in a tone of anguish. "She says it will be wiser, since I am not yet out, to remove me from temptation."

"Not Bodiam again!" protested Tina. "She must know the Duke will not permit her."

"No, this time she plans to send me home to my father's estate in the north. She knows Uncle John has no control there. It is because of the rumors. She thinks she has the better of him at last!"

"What—rumors?" demanded Tina, her heart sinking.

"Gogo came in after dinner last night in high gig. It seems he was told some story about Uncle John which amused him very much, and was not to my uncle's credit, which pleased both of them. Mama sent me from the room at once, but I—ah—lingered in the hallway." Flora gave Tina a defiant look. "I know it was wrong to eavesdrop, but how else is one ever to find out anything? Well, I hid behind that silly suit of armor Mama insists upon keeping by the doorway—the maids hate dusting it; they always knock off some part of it!—and I heard Gogo tell Mama about this house where idle ladies go in the afternoons to meet gentlemen." She frowned. "I'm not sure why that should be so naughty, for surely most males and females of *our order*—as Mama is forever saying!—are idle, and visit one another when not engaged with modistes or hairdressers. Males of course having all the fun, for they have their clubs, and mills, cockfights, and I do not know how many other interesting events!"

"Collect yourself, Flora, and give me a plain tale!" demanded Tina, already deeply apprehensive.

"Well, this house was called the Venus Club, and Gogo told Mama that it was all over town that Uncle John's fiancée—" Flora halted in her tale, her eyes growing rounder as she noticed the horror on Tina's expressive countenance. "—Uncle John's fiancée! But that's *you*, Tina! Gogo's story was about you!" She stared into Tina's white face for a long moment. "It is a lie!" she whispered. "No one will believe it!"

"No one will need to believe it," said Tina quietly. "The harm will be done just by spreading it!"

"What shall we do?" breathed Flora, terrified by the bleak look on the lovely face before her. "We must tell Uncle John at once! Perhaps he can stop Gogo from spreading the story?" Then, as Tina, deep in thought, did not answer, Flora stood up. "I am afraid there is nothing I can do to help you, dearest Tina! Is there?" she added anxiously.

Tina, recalled from her own troubles by the desolation in the face before her, shook her head and forced a smile. "You have proven yourself my friend by coming to me at once with this—this false rumor. Perhaps it is I who should be helping you to endure your situation, but I fear I shall not be able to remain in London if this lie is spread. It will be better also for your uncle if he is not compelled to defend me."

"You will leave London?" faltered the younger girl.

"It may be best to do so." Tina summoned a smile.

"I hate Mama," Flora gritted between small, set teeth. She turned to leave, then came back to give Tina a hard, quick hug. "Thank you for all your kindness to me, Tina. It has been good to be your friend."

Flora left the room hurriedly, crying.

Tina, helpless to assist her, was forced to watch her go.

A quarter of an hour later, while Tina was still trying to decide what was best to do in the situation, and whether Flora's news would change the Duke's strategy, Dolby entered again with a worried look.

"There is a note from your Mama, Miss Athena," he said, offering it upon a small silver tray. "The groom who brought it said it was most urgent—a matter of life and death."

Dolby himself was of the opinion that the groom, youthful and full of his important mission, was milking it for every drop of drama he could squeeze out—but of course it was not Dolby's place to so advise his employer's granddaughter.

Tina took the envelope with dread. The letter was in her mother's hand, so badly scrawled that Tina had difficulty in making out the words. The sum of the disjointed screed seemed to be that Papa had suffered an accident and was lingering at Death's doorway, and could Tina tear herself away from the delights of the London Season and attend her father's bed-side? And be sure to pick up her father's new riding breeches, from their own tailor in Town, since Umphrey would never patronize anyone else, and bring two jars of Restorative Pork Jelly. The two latter requests were heavily underlined.

Tina shook her head in despair. The accident had evidently driven poor Dulcinia out of what little wits she normally employed. If Jase and Killy were away from home, furthering their careers on land and sea, poor little Dulcinia would have no steady support. Gathering her own wits about her, Tina turned to the hovering Dolby.

"It was good of you to wait," she smiled briefly. "This letter was from my mother at Malong Hall. It seems my father has had—an accident, which naturally worries my Mama. She has asked me to return at once to help her. I shall go up and pack a bag, if you, Dolby, will have the small traveling coach made ready?"

"At once, Miss Athena. And your Grandmother?"

Tina hesitated. Then, setting her jaw, she went up to her grandmother's bedroom. Lady Delia, wearing a charming bed-jacket, was lingering over a substantial breakfast.

"Umphrey has had an accident," Tina said baldly. "Mama requires my presence."

"*Not* on the eve of Lady Jersey's Ridotto!" pleaded her grandmother. "Not even *Umphrey* could be that maladroit!"

Wordlessly Tina extended her Mama's letter. Lady Delia perused it, frowning horrendously. "What does she mean, *axehandle*? Oh! that's *accident*. Her spelling is worse than her handwriting! 'Death's hall'—stuff and nonsense! Yet it looks like it: 'Umphrey entering Death's hall' . . . and then something I can't make out; then 'caught and mangled by Death's teeth'! Really, Tina, your Mother is an idiot, although she is my daughter! 'Death's teeth'! Perhaps you get your literary proclivities from Dulcinia." She frowned, sighed, and tapped her finger against the letter before returning it to Tina. "Ring for my maid, please. We shall have to inform the Duke. He will be furious, of course. Your sudden disappearance at this moment will serve to convince all the quizzies that the rumors are true."

"Do we need to tell him?" Tina asked cravenly, and

then answered her own question. "We do, and at once. We must give him time to plan his defense."

"And what of your defense?" challenged Lady Delia.

"It will not so much matter, dear Grandmama, except for its ugly repercussions upon you. You had best disown me publicly, tonight!"

"What do you mean, it won't matter about you?" demanded her grandmother.

"I shall not be returning to London. No," she interrupted her grandmother's protest. "If Father is dying, I shall remain to comfort Mama. You know how she depends upon him . . ." Tina could not go on for a moment. Then she lifted her chin in a shadow of her normal gallantry. "You did your best to make me a success in the Beau Monde, dear Grandmama, but you see it is a hopeless task."

Lady Delia's shoulders drooped. "It was a close-run thing," she sighed. "I nearly brought it off—you and the Duke!"

"He will be relieved, after this storm in a tea-cup has died down," Tina said with a confidence she did not feel. She continued bravely, "He is well rid of a flighty Bluestocking who embroils him in questionable situations and makes him the butt of scandalous *on dits*. He will be glad to be rid of me!"

Lady Delia sighed. "You may be right, child. Even so, you must tell him at once." She glanced at the letter in Tina's hand. "Do you suppose that nodcock wishes to be buried in *riding breeches*?" Catching Tina's anguished glance, she said bruskly, "I do not for one second imagine that your father is at 'Death's door,' Athena. That sounds like Dulcinia—up-in-the-boughs! You will probably discover your parent recovering from a colic! But you must go, dear child. Get dressed. I'll see to all."

Heavy-hearted, Tina agreed. She hugged the old lady gently, and hurried to her own room where her abigail was already packing a small suitcase. Tina changed quickly into a becoming traveling costume in soft amber superfine. Then, taking a lingering look around the pretty room, and resolutely refusing to glance at the Grecian costume the Duke had provided for her—"Heracles— who said Hebe had the power of making him young again." . . . *Oh, John, did you mean it? I have never seen you as too old!*—she turned away.

She took her case from the abigail and went quietly down to the waiting carriage. At least she would see him this once more, and perhaps—

Tom Coachman, wearing a lugubrious expression, received her instructions to stop at Renfrew House on his way out of London with open relief. Did *everyone* know? But of course, Tina reminded herself. The trip did not seem half long enough. Tina had not yet decided how to present her news when one of the Duke's footmen was handing her out of the carriage and through the front door. There Cullon met her with a Friday face.

"His Grace has been called away on a matter of great urgency, Miss Long," the butler said. "I have already despatched a messenger to Lady Camden's home with the news. Miss Flora has disappeared again," he concluded, sharply aware of her shocked and desolate expression. "His Grace was most concerned that you should lack his support at the Ridotto this Friday. He hoped to be back in London before that important event. But you will find his sentiments and his—ah—suggestions in the note he has sent to Lady Camden's home, Miss Long."

"I wish to leave this for His Grace," said Tina dully, holding out the message from her mother. "Please inform His Grace that my father is gravely ill and I am summoned to Malong Hall. I am leaving at once."

Cullon was obviously unhappy at this turn of events, and apprehensive that his master would be angry with him for not persuading Miss Long to remain in London, but he had no choice. He attended the young lady back to her carriage as though she were royalty. He was dismayed to note that she was crying as the coach drew off.

Chapter 14

As Lady Delia's carriage rolled smoothly over the roads toward Malong Hall, a miserable Tina had plenty of time to consider her situation. At least John would not think she had been running away from the scandal in a craven way—her mother's letter would prove that point. But what had occurred to take him from London so precipitately? Could he have changed his mind, and decided to challenge either or both of the vicious rumor-mongers to a duel? If Flora's incoherent account was true, the wicked lies were being spread all over London. Even if he succeeded in silencing the sources of the canard, the ugly story would spread in all directions, like waves from a rock thrown in a pond.

Flora! In her own misery, Tina had forgotten poor little Flora. Perhaps someday, if she became a noted writer, she might try to find the child again and offer friendship. At that thought, Tina's mouth twisted in self-condemnation. She had not been of much assistance to the young girl, running away when her friendship was the only thing Flora had to cling to. Where was Flora?

By the time Tom Coachman decided to stop to rest his team and get Miss Long refreshment, Tina's mind was exhausted with fruitless schemes and her heart was sore with regret. For she had finally faced the truth—that she was deeply, recklessly, hopelessly in love with a man who saw her only as a greedy opportunist; "so determined a campaigner for marital bliss," he had accused her. She remembered every word he had spoken to her. Unfortunately, the sting of contempt behind most of them still hurt as much as it had originally done.

What was worse, she had invited his scorn by answering his question of why she had come to London with bald honesty, admitting she came to find a husband. Of course he had been disgusted! Perhaps if she had also confessed her plan to have her teaching manual published, he might have given her the benefit of some delicacy of feeling? But no! Her avowed purpose was one completely without delicacy, and must be such as would disgust any man of sensibility and taste! Tina groaned and wished she had it to do over. London was a forcing-bed for maturity. Was it too late for her?

Rallying enough to put on a brighter face for Tom Coachman, she dismounted at his command and allowed him to accompany her into the genteel inn at which, he informed her, Lady Delia always stopped for refreshment. It appeared he was known, and favorably known, here. Tina found herself cosseted and treated with every courtesy. She forced herself to eat something from several of the dishes she was offered; the result was a lightening of her black mood. She returned to the carriage much strengthened, and began to consider the situation at Malong Hall.

Was Papa really seriously ill? Mama's frenzied letter would seem to indicate that he was, but a long association with that scatter-brained female had taught Tina to look for the small grain of truth within the dramatic presentation. For example: there was the underlined request for Umphrey's new riding breeches. Why should Dulcinia be so urgent about such a minor and actually useless detail, if her husband were on his death-bed? And then there was the Restorative Jelly. Sighing, the girl realized she would have to wait until she reached Malong Hall before she could find the answers she sought.

It was well after dusk when Tom Coachman brought the carriage to a halt in a well-lighted yard behind a rather imposing inn. He helped her down and she was glad of his arm. Several hours in a coach, no matter how well-sprung, tended to stiffen muscles unaccustomed to such rigors.

"This is where Lady Camden usually spends the night when on the road to your parents' home," he advised her, and led her into the pleasant hallway. Here Mine Host and his wife made her welcome with discreet warmth, and the buxom lady led her up to a pleasant bedroom where a small fire burned on the hearth and the bed was already turned down.

"You will wish to have a supper before you retire," suggested the hostess firmly. "There is a private parlour which Lady Camden always uses. Your meal will be ready for you in half an hour."

"Thank you," said Tina, too tired to argue the matter.

She washed her face and combed her shining hair into some sort of order, then wondered if she would even bother to go down to the parlour. It was in her mind that she should be driving on through the night, to reach Malong Hall as rapidly as possible, but the memory of the coachman's tired elderly face restrained her. Had she enough money to hire a relief-coachman? Surely old Tom could not object to that! Tina counted, the coins and notes in her reticule, and decided that there might be enough. Of course there was the expense of the inns, and the meals for both of them. She would ask that Tom be brought to her after dinner, and discuss the matter honestly with him. A little more comfortable for this decision, Tina left her cozy bedroom and went along the hallway toward the head of the stairs.

Suddenly she halted. From behind one of the closed doors came a wisp of sound—a woman's sobbing. Tina took two more steps toward the stairs, then paused. The sound came again: the heartbroken cry of a woman in deep grief. Tina went back and tapped softly on the panel.

The sobbing ceased abruptly. There was a pause so long that Tina was afraid the other woman was going to ignore the knocking. Then a very young voice called out unsteadily, "Who is it?"

With a thrill of fear and hope, Tina identified the childish voice. She opened the door and slipped quietly inside, closing it after her.

Flora raised a puffy red face from the pillow. Her eyes widened with surprise and then the whole small, tragic face came to life.

"Tina! Is it really you? Oh, *Tina*!"

The older girl came quickly to the bed and took the sobbing child in her arms. "you are safe now, my dear," she crooned softly. "You can come home with me until we decide what to do about your problem."

Flora's head came up warily. "Home?"

"I am on my way to Malong Hall. You will be most welcome there for as long as your Mama will permit you to stay."

"I shall not tell her where I am!" cried Flora. "She really does not care. She only uses me to hurt Uncle John."

"While we are thinking about that, why do we not share

147

a very good dinner which I am assured is waiting for us in the private parlour?" coaxed Tina. "I know I am hungry. Are not you?"

Flora gave a watery smile. "Ravenous," she admitted. "I did not have money for both a room and food, so I told the innkeeper I was not hungry. I came by stage-coach—"

"But where were you going?" asked Tina. Time enough to scold her for the alarm, the fears her unannounced departure had given rise to. For now, she must be comforted. Tina smiled lovingly into the pale little face with its frame of bright red hair still bouncing defiantly. "What was your plan?"

"I was going to Renfrew Keep," she admitted. "I knew—*no one*—could get me away from there without Uncle John's permission. He is Head of the house, you know," she added naïvely. "It is his Castle."

Tina hugged her. "You were right to place your dependence upon your uncle," she said softly, "and you did let *him* know where you were going—"

The sudden appalled expression on the child's countenance halted Tina in mid-sentence. "Flora! You left him a message, surely?"

The bright red head shook guiltily. "No. I forgot."

Tina hugged her once more, but a look of decision had taken the place of sympathy. "We must let him know at once. I'll ask Tom Coachman to send a groom post-haste. They will all be beside themselves with anxiety."

"Mama will not," objected Flora stubbornly. "I do not wish her to be told where I am."

"She will use your defection as a whip for the Duke's shoulders," Tina advised, grimly.

"You care for Uncle John, do you not?" ventured Flora, her pale little countenance alight with affection and curiosity. "I *do* love you, Tina! I am so pleased you are going to be my Aunt!"

Tina, feeling the treacherous warmth in her own breast, made haste to get the child to her feet and over to the commode to wash the tear stains from her cheeks. It would not do, she thought, holding a towel for the now happily splashing Flora, to discuss her feelings about the impassive Duke, nor his for her. Her immediate concern was to get this child to safety somewhere. She found herself unexpectedly angry at a family whose older members were so irresponsible in their behavior toward the children. Her own family, though not over-endowed with brains, were warm and loving, and cared for each other's happiness.

She led the now contented Flora down to dinner in the small private parlour. The meal was a good one, and both girls did it justice. Then, not wishing to linger near the public rooms of the inn, Tina took Flora back to her room. She explained the situation when both girls were comfortable beside the tiny fire.

"My Mama has written me a letter saying that my Papa is at Death's door," she began. "But there are mitigating circumstances."

Flora, at once entranced at the drama thus unfolded to her, clasped her hands and waited, open-mouthed.

Tina took a breath and continued. "You should understand that my family are the dearest, most loving people in the world, but they tend to—to lack *judgment*. My mother especially is moved to extremes of emotion upon very little provocation—"

"You mean she goes up into the boughs at the slightest excuse," nodded Flora. "Or even without one."

Tina chuckled. "You sound as though you knew her!"

Flora said simply, "My Cousin Harriet is such an one. She goes into a *flusteration* over matters which anyone else would see no need to bother about. She seems to enjoy being in a frenzy."

Although the picture was not totally acceptable, Tina let it go, since it saved further explanations. "Mama says in her letter—or *seems* to say," she corrected herself, "since her handwriting is atrocious and she crosses her lines not once but several times, and has afterthoughts which she writes in along the margins!—at all events, she seems to be saying that Papa is desperately ill, dying, in fact, and then she commands me—underlined!—to bring with me to Malong Hall his new riding breeches and two jars of Restorative Pork Jelly!"

"Perhaps her doctor has told them to expect a miracle?" suggested Flora. Then she frowned. "But why the breeches? Unless your Papa had expressed a wish to be—that is," Flora's face turned scarlet. "Do forgive me, Tina! You are such a *comfortable listener* that I do not realize the implications of what I am saying!" She hung her head.

Tina rose, went to the child, and hugged her warmly. "That is the finest thing you could have told me," she said softly. "Yes, it is possible that my dear Papa might have expressed a wish to be buried in his new breeches, but there was something about Mama's letter which puzzles me. I must tell you that Mama is not in the least bookish or romantic, yet in the letter she said something to the effect that my father had been 'caught and mangled by Death's teeth'! Such fustian is not in her way at all!"

"It sounds," said Flora judiciously, "as though he'd been attacked by a horse. Have you one by that name— Death?—in your stables?"

Tina stared at the child with open mouth. *Out of the mouths of babes—!* Entering *Death's hall* now translated to *Death's stall*. And if Umphrey's riding breeches had been "caught and mangled by Death's teeth," of course he would be anxious for their replacement. Suddenly a gurgle of laughter rose in her throat and would not be denied.

She began to laugh so heartily that Flora, at first startled, soon joined in the fun. They shook with laughter, gasping as the fit left them. Tina beamed fondly at Flora.

"That was more Restorative than Pork Jelly," she announced, sending the younger girl into another fit of giggles.

Tina smiled fondly at her. "Now, I have a proposal to make—two, in fact. I shall send off a note to the Duke at once, informing him of your presence with me. That should allay the worst of his alarm," she added hopefully. "Then, tomorrow, you will accompany me in my grandmother's coach—much more comfortable than the stage, and certainly less expensive!—to Malong Hall, where we will discover if indeed my Papa has lost an argument with a new horse named Death."

Since Flora regarded Tina's plans as inspired, both girls went off to bed in good spirits. They got an early start the following morning. Tom Coachman was plainly worried at the presence of a new passenger—and that one a daughter of the notorious shrew Lady Rate, but was somewhat reassured since Miss Long had sent off a message to the Duke. If he pushed the horses, he could get his two charges to Malong Hall within two days, which meant only one more night on the road, tempting Fate that no one would recognize either of the girls and spread scandal. Tom sighed. It was not easy being the guardian of Young Females. He really had not had the training for it.

The following evening, after a long, exhausting day in the carriage, the girls ate quietly at the inn Tom Coachman selected, and Flora went thankfully upstairs to the room the girls shared. Tina, equally tired, felt she had to write to her grandmother, which duty she had unaccountably forgotten in her concern with her letter to the Duke. She was just nicely launched into a lengthy and detailed account of the last two days when she was disturbed by loud voices in the hallway, one imperious, the other obsequious, followed by the beat of furious footsteps along the uncarpeted hallway to the private parlour. The door was thrust open and the Duke of Renfrew, magnificent in riding dress, strode into the room, immediately making it seem tiny and crowded by his presence.

The nobleman was obviously in a fury. Gone was the normal cool impassivity of his expression, the faintly arrogant imperturbability which had, upon occasion, annoyed Tina to the point of exasperation. Instead she was confronted by a dark Corsair, whose eyes blazed with anger. Directed at herself! Tina opened her mouth, gasped, and closed it cravenly.

The Duke nodded. "Wise of you!" His voice rose as he went on, "You idiot! You little coward! How dared you leave London without telling me?"

Tina's scattered wits were collecting themselves at the injustice of the Duke's attack. "How could I tell you? You were gone!"

"I was trying to find that idiot niece of mine! Sophia drove her away and she's disappeared! But I counted— foolishly, as it appears!—upon *you* to hold the fort for me in London, not to slink away like a dismissed servant at the first sign of danger!"

Tina's rage at these unjust charges was almost as great as His Grace's by this time. "I went to your home to tell you that my father was said to be dying—! You must know that! I left Mother's letter for you to read—"

"As soon as I returned to London from Bodiam, where I was sure I'd find Flora, I was given your Mother's letter." That seemed to enrage him further. "She is more idiotic than you are! I rode post-haste to Malong Hall, where I thought I would find you. You seem to set a very slow pace for one supposedly rushing to a death-bed!"

"My father!" demanded Tina quickly. "Is he really ill?"

A reluctant smile tugged briefly at the Duke's stern lips. "He has a broken leg and a badly lacerated posterior. His new stallion bears the provocative name of Death." He watched Tina's expressive little face intently, grinning in sympathy at her dawning understanding. "He had opened the door of Death's stall, startling the mettlesome beast into attack, which included biting him after knocking him down."

Tina nodded. "So that's why Mama was so insistent upon my bringing the new riding breeches—which I forgot to pick up in my haste to get to his death-bed!" She began to chuckle.

He joined her laughter, but after a minute a darkling shadow crossed his face. "Do you chance to know where Flora went? Now I've got you safe under my hand, I suppose we shall have to search for the brat. Of all the *idiots*!" It seemed to be a word much in his mind.

"She's upstairs in my bedroom," Tina informed him casually. She was still thinking about his phrase *got you safe under my hand*.

Instead of the relief and gratitude she was entitled to expect, the Duke glared at her with renewed anger.

"Upstairs—! You mean you *helped* her to run away from her home? Encouraged her in her childish rebellion? Failed to notify anyone as to her whereabouts? You irresponsible little lunatic, I've set the Bow Street Runners after her!"

Tina gasped. The Duke must indeed have been concerned for the young girl, alone and miserable and frightened, prey to any scoundrel she might encounter. With understanding came gentleness, and Tina rose and went quickly to the angry giant. Placing her hand on his arm, she said softly, "She's well, and quite over the unhappiness which drove her from her mother's house—"

The Duke interrupted with an icy glare of distaste, "Spare me your comforting platitudes, if you please! Take me to Flora at once!" Tina snatched away her hand from the iron bar of his arm and glared back at him with equal distaste. "Why should I? So that you can shout and sneer at the girl, and bullock her as you have been doing with me? I think not, Your Grace! She is tired and she's gone to bed. Where I am going to join her!"

The Duke caught her arm and drew her back to the sofa by the fireplace. "Simmer down, little fire-eater." He made her sit down and, after pulling the bell-rope, he sat beside her. Tina glared at him, but the fire had indeed gone out of her as she observed, at this closer vantage point, the lines of exhaustion which marked his dark face. He had been on the stretch with apprehension for Flora's safety, and had made a forced ride down to Malong Hall in Tina's behalf—surely out of character for the arrogant, unfeeling nobleman! And now he had found her, after stopping no doubt at every respectable inn on the road back to London, to reassure her as to Umphrey Long's well-being! No wonder the poor man was weary. He could even be excused for feeling scornful at the stupidities of those who surrounded him, who depended upon his strength and decision to keep them out of the worst sort of muddles into which they seemed always to be falling!

Very much in charity with her arrogant nobleman, Tina longed to smooth away the lines from the strong face and offer whatever sort of comfort and solace he wished.

The Duke glanced up from the fire and caught the softened glow in Tina's wide golden eyes. At once his own eyes narrowed with interest, and his expression acquired a distinctly predatory look. For some reason this did not alarm Tina. She smiled into his hard countenance, and said softly, "How much we all owe Your Grace! It is unfeeling of us to dump all our problems into your lap!

But you are unfailingly good! A wise elder counselor!"

The dark piratical eyebrows rose sharply. Then his lips widened into a wolfish grin. "What are you up to, witch? This sudden excess of mawkish amiability must have some dark purpose behind it. Soothing syrup and sentimentality! Are you practicing for the composition of a romantic novel?"

Tina's hackles rose at his taunting mockery. Devil that he was, he did not permit the expression of even common courtesy without voicing his suspicions of the speaker's bona fides! She hated him!

The creature was looking at her with his eyes glinting with amusement. Tina suppressed her fury and disappointment sternly. Whatever she might have been moved to say was forever lost as the Host entered and asked their pleasure.

"I shall have a meal, whatever your good wife can prepare for me. The best wine in your cellar. A glass of something suitable for this lady, who has already eaten, I am given to understand. While I am dining, a bedchamber to be prepared for me. I think that is all for the present."

Bowing and smiling, the inn-keeper got himself out of the room. Tina regarded the Duke with a jaundiced eye.

"You are very sure of yourself, are you not?" she said.

The Duke only shrugged.

"Does everyone always do exactly as you wish?" she persisted.

The big man raised one eyebrow. "Yes."

Tina felt the rising of fury within her once more. She had to get out of this room before she found herself yelling at her tormentor like a fishwife. Well, she could leave now; he was in the way of being fed and rested without need of any comfort she could give. She opened her mouth to bid him a chilly good night.

The devil forestalled her. "I wish," he said in a voice

notable for its absence of arrogance, "that you would remain for just a few minutes, share a glass of wine with me, and tell me what has been happening. We have much to discuss," he finished, in a wheedling voice. *"Athena?"*

Tina felt like a child's ball, bouncing back and forth on its string at the whim of the owner. First the Duke treated her with contempt, driving her from him; then coaxed her back with appeals to her compassion and courtesy. She frowned at him.

"I do not see what we have to talk about," she stated repressively.

The Duke's boyish grin disarmed her. "You are just saying that because I was cross with you. Being worried, tired, and hungry at the time." He tried to adopt a pathetic mien.

Tina felt a rush of automatic compassion, as quickly doused when she noted his sideways glance to see how she was taking his wheedle. "You are a thimble-rigger, a Captain Sharp, sir! What do you want of me?"

"Merely to talk, to plan our campaign, Athena," the Duke coaxed. The entrance of the host and two serving girls with His Grace's meal and the wines forced the end to private conversation, but when, at length, they were alone again, Tina found it hard to maintain her querulous attitude. He looked so very tired, and he ate his dinner like a starving man.

"When did you last eat?" she demanded.

The Duke shrugged. "Late last night. Your charming Mama insisted that I break my fast, although the hour was so advanced."

"You mean she did not give you breakfast this morning?"

"I stayed at the inn near your home. It would not," the Duke advised her primly, "have been *convenable* for me to stay in a house of mourning." He glanced at her sideways. A most reprehensible look, Tina fumed. What was he playing at? One would almost think the wretched creature was enjoying her company, and attempting some sort of light-hearted dalliance!

The girl sighed. He was irresistible in this role, and he knew it.

"Talk!" she commanded.

The Duke chuckled, wiped his mouth neatly, and began.

"I explained to your Mama about Lady Jersey's Ridotto tomorrow night, and how *necessary* it is for you to attend. I did not need to mention the importance of scotching the scurrilous lies of the two men who saw you in Fort Street. It was enough to hint at the possibility of securing a voucher for Almack's. Your Mama—although she hardly looks it—is more than seven!

"She informed me with charming naïveté that she and your family had despaired of your making a success in the Beau Monde—*since you had shown absolutely no interest in obtaining a husband*, in spite of their combined efforts. Lady C. was their last resort."

He laughed aloud at the repulsive look which crossed Tina's face at this disclosure. "Ah, my love, if ever I need to know the truth of your statements, I shall consult Lady Dulcinia!"

Tina was so struck by the casual sweetness of his *my love* that she forgot to be angry at his shameless pumping of her Mama.

"What else did she tell you?"

"Very little that I had not already deduced," smiled the Duke. "*I*, in turn, assured *her* that you were a tremendous success and would undoubtedly receive at least one distinguished offer after Lady Jersey's ball—*if you were able to be there!* At which she urged me to find you, somewhere on the road between Malong Hall and London, and bear you back post-haste to Lady Camden."

"You are a ruthless man," said Tina. "Did you identify the gentleman who was to make me the distinguished offer?"

"No," replied the Duke with a prim mouth, "I did not become specific."

"Just as well," snapped Tina. "I am not returning to London."

"Why not?" demanded the Duke coldly. "Are you afraid of a little gossip? Or are you avenging yourself upon me because I accused you of tricking me into marriage? I have announced our betrothal publicly. You know enough about Society to realize that it will be impossible for me to withdraw now, and humiliating to be forced to explain your absence. Is it your desire that I be so embarrassed?"

Tina clenched her hands into small fists. "You have not thought of the effects of my presence upon your own dignity, Your Grace! I have no desire to embarrass you. My presence in London will encourage your sister to spread her lies. But when I fail to return, surely the sympathy of the *Ton* will be with you, deluded victim of a scheming female, and the story will soon be forgotten?"

"If you think I wish to be known as the tottyheaded victim of a scheming minx, you are far off! And you have apparently forgotten that your Grandmother will be deeply hurt, perhaps even ostracised by your defection." He frowned at her anxious little face. "Can you not trust me and your Grandmama to pull all the chestnuts out of the fire? Come, show a little courage, Athena! Trust me, and you shall achieve your heart's desire!"

Tina felt the stirrings of hope. "What would you have me do, Your Grace?"

"Merely accept the fact that you have achieved every girl's objective in coming to London: to catch a husband," grinned the Duke.

"But as my too-confiding Mama informed you, it was not by choice that I entered upon this quest. In short, sir, I do not want a husband! I never did!"

"Yet you lent yourself to the plan, and came to the Marriage Mart with Lady Camden," said the Duke sternly. "What was your reason?"

Tina shrugged. "I disliked the notion of dwindling into an ape-leader. Perhaps I was even jealous of a red-haired flirt who had all the youths in the county at her feet. Or perhaps I was bored with the dulness of conversation which concerned itself solely with horses and hunting and county gossip."

"But surely bucolic conversation has not suddenly risen to new heights of sparkling interest?"

"No, I am sure it has not. But the sale of my manual, of which I told you, has convinced me that I can find more real satisfaction in creative activity than in the idle life of a society matron." Catching his look of incredulity, Tina added quickly, "I am to do several more books for the same purchaser. I shall be well-occupied and happy, I assure you."

"You will not miss the dances, and concerts, the theater?"

"All these can be found outside London," prevaricated Tina, annoyed at his persistence. "Malong Hall is not Outer Mongolia, you know!"

"Near enough," said the Duke, unforgivably. He lifted one haughty eyebrow at her. "I have listened with patience to your arguments, Athena. I have decided, however, that I need you in London."

"You need me—?" Tina found herself echoing.

"Yes. As I told your Mama, I shall take you and Flora

back to London with me. I shall keep Flora in my Town House, employ a governess until she can be enrolled in a good school which will challenge her growing mind. You will continue to be her friend, and accompany her on our educational trips as long as she is in the city. And Friday night—why, that is tomorrow, is it not?—we shall attend the Ridotto together."

As he made these arrogant announcements, Tina found herself torn between anger and incredulous joy. She was forced to admit that whatever his reasons, she wanted to be with this overbearing, beautiful man wherever, whenever, he wished. Unable to voice further objections, she said, "I am tired," in a cross little voice.

The Duke opened the parlour door for her, bowed, and watched her progress as she slowly mounted the stairs.

Chapter 15

Tina's feelings were mixed as she prepared for Lady Jersey's Ridotto. The costume the Duke had provided for her was at once daring and demure, a white-and-gold enchantment of softly draped material and subtly placed gold cord. For the first time in her life, her lack of inches was disguised—or made unimportant—by the artful fall of silken material. With her crown of dark, shining hair she was, in fact, a tiny goddess.

In spite of her own, Hugget's, and Lady Delia's delighted recognition of her beautiful turnout, Tina was still very frightened. Lady Sophia had not communicated with her, or her grandmother; the Duke had sent masses of flowers and some charming trifles (a fillet of flexible gold to crown her coiffure in the Grecian style, and a flexible golden necklace set with glowing topaz), but no message had accompanied the gifts. So it was impossible for Tina to know what plans His Grace had made to get them out of the social ruin which threatened. Grandmama, appealed to in desperation, merely shook her head and advised Tina to trust the Duke.

Trust the Duke! Of course she did! But then how could even so skilled a social campaigner as he was get them out of this tangled web of malice and hatred? Taking a last glance at the surprisingly lovely little figure in the mirror, Tina squared her shoulders and prepared to enter the arena.

We who are about to die, salute you! she thought wryly, echoing the famous salutation of Roman gladiators before the Games.

When she joined Lady Delia, Tina was encouraged by the impressive picture her Grandmama presented. In a superb representation of a Greek Matron, Lady Delia positively glowed with restrained magnificence. Her robe was of so dark a purple as to look almost black in some lights, and her famous rubies burned with autocratic splendor at throat, wrist, fingers and upon her snowy hair. Tina began to feel more confident.

"We make a handsome pair," she smiled.

"It is more important that you and Renfrew make a handsome pair," corrected Lady Delia.

"And that he does not catch cold," Tina could not forbear adding. "The ancient Greeks really had no inhibitions about displaying their—ah—manly charms."

Lady Delia, who liked a salted reference if it were not crudely expressed, smothered a smile.

At this moment, a footman announced the arrival of the Duke, and both ladies went down to the drawing room to join him. Tina caught her breath at sight of him.

He always stood head and shoulders above most of the company, but tonight there was a blazing splendor about John Stone which dazzled the eye. His six-foot-four inches were draped in a short linen tunic with a metal breast-plate whose bosses caught the light. A short, very practical looking broadsword hung from a leather belt at his narrow waist. The pleated tunic fell just above his knees, revealing powerfully muscled legs. A cloak of royal purple was caught over one massive shoulder with a jewelled clasp, and above it rose the strong wide column of His Grace's throat and the noble, darkly handsome head. Tina experienced a strange weakness in her knees which had the odd effect of rendering her breathless. It was left for Lady Delia to say, "Incomparable, John! If any other man in London could carry off such barbaric magnificence, you would start a fashion tonight!"

The Duke smiled. His eyes went to Tina, and lingered over her delicate beauty. "Perhaps we all might set a new style—if the English climate more closely resembled the Mediterranean." He could not seem to stop staring at Tina. "Athena," he said softly. "I think it should have been Aphrodite!"

This remark enabled Tina to regain her voice. "But there is already an Aphrodite Long, sir. My beautiful sister! A 'Goddess, excellently bright,' as Ben Jonson wrote," she concluded, with a naughty glance at Lady Delia.

The Duke cut in smoothly before her grandmother had a chance to express displeasure. "But you are not prepared to flaunt your blue stockings this evening, I see." His eyes went boldy over her figure, lingering on the shapely legs under the revealing close-drape of her costume. Lady Delia suppressed a huff of laughter, and Tina felt herself coloring under that predatory glance. She held her head proudly.

"Indeed not, Your Grace," she retorted pertly. "I shall, in fact, attempt to captivate every male creature at the ball!"

Her rebellion, if such it was, was quickly quelled. "I think not," said His Grace smoothly, moving forward and taking her arm in fingers of iron. "I believe I must instruct you in the proper strategy. The primary purpose of this evening's exercise is to secure your voucher for Almack's—the symbol of your acceptance by the Beau Monde. To this end, we must scotch the vile rumors already set about by my wretched sister, her son, and the two libertines who observed you on Fort Street. I have contrived a plan."

When he did not continue, Lady Delia prodded, "What is it? And what roles do you wish us to play?"

"Yourselves," said the Duke firmly. "Only that. Allow me to direct the action."

Tina scanned the magnificently virile man beside her. The Grecian trappings, while enhancing his powerful male body, were not solely responsible for the impression he made. It came to her that John Stone, Duke of Renfrew, would stand out in any costume, in any group of men. He had bred true to those qualities which had first won the Dukedom. For all his arrogance, if any man could resolve their dangerous problem, it was John Stone.

Partly to cover her extreme admiration, partly to express it, Tina said in rallying tones, "For myself, I intend to behave as though you were my whole dependence and delight—as the phrase is."

"Do so," invited the Duke with his wide wolfish smile. "It will be good practice for you," and he offered an arm to each lady and led them out to his carriage.

Their arrival at Lady Jersey's home was in the nature of a royal progress. Even the crowds of the *hoi polloi*, gathered in the street to gawk at the swells in their colorful costumes, received the Duke's party with cries of admiration, and when a footman handed down a small black boy in an elaborate costume, there was vociferous applause.

"Whatever is that?" questioned Tina, but the Duke merely took her arm and her grandmother's and escorted them into the wide hallway, lit with a thousand candles and crowded with members of the *Ton*. A hasty glance to the rear showed Tina that the child was following them, bearing a shining package.

Sally Jersey, heading her own reception line at the top of the wide stairway, cried out with delight at their costumes, and bade them an extravagant welcome. She herself was charmingly pert as Columbine. When the Duke's ladies had expressed their greetings, the Duke waved forward the little black page.

"A trifling gift for you, my dear Sally," he said gently.

Lady Jersey's eyes widened as they took in the richly dressed small figure. "In the nature of a bribe, perhaps?" she taunted sweetly. It was clear she had heard the rumors.

The Duke favored her with what Tina privately thought to be a devastating smile. "For you, my dear? Absolutely useless to try any such ploy upon one of your acknowledged *nous*! No, Aladdin is merely the bearer of a real gift for you. Miss Long and I know how well one of your brightness of mind will appreciate it. It comes from *Fort Street*." He enunciated the contentious name clearly.

There was a sudden silence, and then the hiss of drawn breaths, as all those who had been pretending not to listen to the exchange between the two powerful social arbiters now gaped openly.

Sally Jersey's eyes assessed the gold-foil-wrapped package the black page was offering her. Then curiosity won, and she accepted it and tore away the wrappings.

To Tina's complete astonishment, a small book in a bright orange cover was revealed.

Lady Sally stared at it. "*Roads to Wonder*? What is this, Renfrew?"

The Duke took Tina's hand and pulled her closer to

himself and Lady Jersey. "My fiancée—who has really dreaded being revealed as a Bluestocking!—has just had this most useful volume published by Guthrie and Sinclair, in *Fort Street*. It is already a success in the field for which she intended it, but she is of such overweening modesty that she has refused to permit any advertisement of her work." He grinned at Lady Jersey. "Feeling that *I* might—er—cut up rough!" He joined the general laugh at his sudden descent into cant.

Lady Jersey's eyes were bright with admiration and amusement. "My dear Renfrew, you should have been a General! You have cut the ground out from under your enemies' feet! So charmingly, too! I hope you are going to permit me to keep this pretty page? As I recall, my own Mama had one very like him to attend upon her!"

The Duke bowed. "He is yours! And Athena and I hope you will be pleased to bestow your patronage upon her work. We shall pen a most flattering and obsequious dedication to be included with the text, if you will permit? I assure you, the work is scholarly."

Sally Jersey handed back the volume to the waiting page. "Aladdin shall keep it until I have time to peruse it! I am not very—*scholarly* myself, but it would be flattering to become a patron of the arts!" She gave Tina two fingers to shake, bestowed a smile upon her, and turned to the next guests in line.

None of the three spoke until they were safely within the ballroom. Then Lady Delia smiled up at the Duke. "Thank you, John! That was masterly!"

He smiled and pressed her hand where it lay on his forearm.

"Renfrew protects its own," he said. "It is our family motto."

Tina felt again that strange weakness at the knees and the accompanying breathlessness.

At this moment the musicians struck up a lively tune. Since this was a Ridotto, with all the guests in masquerade, there was none of the careful formality that usually marked a Grand Ball. It was hard to single out the most important personages when everyone was hiding under an assumed identity. Many of the dancers were masked. A few even had elaborate constructions over their entire heads to represent strange beings. Under such conditions, the rules of precedence could hardly be enforced.

Establishing Lady Delia with a gaggle of her cronies, the Duke swung Tina out onto the floor to join the waltzing couples. The girl had been hoping for just this moment.

"Thank you, John! It was a splendid stratagem!" she beamed.

The Duke held her a little closer and said softly, "I think Sally Jersey accepted it. And she is such a talker that the word will be in everyone's ear before the evening ends, and all over London tomorrow. Sophia and George are thwarted, and the two spies discredited. Yes, it was a good evening's work, but we had to pay for it by branding you a Bluestocking. Do you regret it?"

Tina's head rose proudly. "I glory in it! The day will come when everyone will receive a good general education, and with it the power to make something worthwhile of himself! How could I regret my small part in that?"

"But the Polite World is hardly ready for pedagogical revolution, my dear Athena," interjected the Duke smoothly. "Nor will it welcome a militant Bluestocking, manning a barricade of text-books!"

"Much I care," muttered Tina. "I shall be happily writing my manuals and possibly even setting up a school of my own at Malong Hall!"

The Duke's shout of laughter attracted attention. He softened his voice as he said, "Can you not picture Dulcinia and Umphrey acting as sponsors for such a school? They will commit you to Bedlam first!"

"I may not go back there," Tina retorted. Now that John had smoothed her path and confounded the gossips, she might just stay in London with Lady Delia and enjoy the cultural amenities of the metropolis. She said as much.

"And our engagement?" challenged the Duke.

Her eyes were wide and troubled as she stared up into his face. "You have done so much for me, Your Grace! Of course your comfort must be my first concern!"

"My comfort?" repeated the Duke, as though he did not particularly enjoy the taste of the words. "I recall that you once called me a *wise elder counselor*, and upon another occasion, thanked me for my middle-aged indulgence of you children. How great *is* the gap between us, Athena?"

"I am nineteen," she admitted, feeling very green and gauche in the presence of his wordly self-possession.

"And I am thirty-six, twice your age and one hundred times your experience." His voice was somber, repressive. Tina felt suddenly cut off and lonely—rejected as unworthy by every criterion. She peered up at him as he swung her deftly among the other dancers.

"We owe you so much, Lady Delia and I," she began, in a small humble voice.

The Duke caught her uncomfortably close and then held her away from him. His dark, saturnine face looked down at her, impassive and arrogant. "Yes, you do owe me rather a lot," he said, surprisingly. "I will tell you how I intend to collect the debt."

Tina waited, the beginnings of alarm stirring in her breast.

After a long pause, the Duke said, in a voice whose silken menace sent a chill of fear through the girl, "First: your behavior tonight must be that of a young woman joyously approaching a much-to-be-desired wedding."

His fine eyes mocked her troubled face. "Can you manage that, do you think, Athena?"

"Yes," the girl answered simply. If only he knew how eagerly she longed to be the arrogant Duke's bride!

"You will not betray, by word or deed, that our engagement is—a hoax. You will continue to partner me at whatever social events I choose. You are a very effective buffer against encroaching females."

Tina felt her anger rising at this cynical pronouncement. She bit back the retort which rose to her lips. The Duke, holding her effortlessly close to his body, watched the changing expressions which passed across the little face. He nodded. "I see you are learning to control your tongue and your temper," he goaded. "By the end of the Season, I shall have schooled you well enough to make you desirable to other men."

This was too much. No female, however grateful, could be expected to put up with weeks of such deflating remarks. More bitterly than she herself was aware, Tina struck back at her tormentor. "Who would want another man's cast-off—even if the other man was a Duke?"

His grip tightened painfully. "You are repudiating the bargain?" his voice was hard.

"Of course not! I asked a simple question," Tina defied him.

The Duke's smile was an insult. "Almost any man in the *Ton*—if I am the Duke referred to in your *simple question*. I am known to be most particular, fastidious, and experienced."

"Your Grace should open a School for Concubines!" flamed Tina, prey to emotions she had never felt before.

"Be careful, Athena! You are casting down the gauntlet! I never refuse a dare."

He was mocking her! The girl threw back her head to confront him face to face.

The Duke seized the opportunity. Placing his hard mouth over hers, he kissed her until she was breathless, dizzy, and stumbling. Forgotten was the crowded ballroom around them. Forgotten Lady Delia and decorum, Lady Jersey, Almack's, and the sharp eyes and sharper tongues of the quizzes. When the Duke finally lifted his dark corsair's head from hers, Tina gasped. She was conscious of one warm, hard hand firm against the nape of her slender neck. She was aware of a fire running along her veins, and the trembling of her knees—which seemed to be almost a permanent state when she was with the Duke. Her great golden eyes blazed up into his.

"No wonder mankind has committed every possible folly in the name of Love," she said, voicing her inmost thoughts.

The predatory smile widened on his Grace's beautiful mouth. "No wonder?" he prodded.

Tina was too dazed by her experience to have her guard up against this man. "It is magic . . . cataclysmic . . . the earth whirls! It is even more powerful than the other time—"

The freest, most delighted laugh she had yet heard from the Duke's lips rang out. All he said, however, was, "You are an apt pupil, Athena." He kept his arms about her, steadying her, his great shoulders a shield against prying eyes, until she had regained her breath and her balance.

Tina found her cheek pressing against metal. She drew back slightly and dared to look up into his face again. He was smiling a gentler smile than she had ever seen upon his lips. And then he said, "Do you think you could become addicted to my love-making, Athena?"

Tina blushed a fiery red under that amused scrutiny. She was being brought back too quickly from her romantic revelation. For a few precious moments it had seemed as though all problems were solved, all questions answered; as though she were on the verge of knowing some profound truth which would cast its light upon all her days. His words brought her back to reality—the crowded ballroom, the overheated air thick with perfumes, the noise of the orchestra and the people talking above it.

"I would like to go home," said Tina.

At once the spell was broken and the Duke's face returned to its wonted impassivity. "We shall remain until after supper. You have obviously forgotten our reason for being here."

The dancing continued. Tina was never left alone. Sometimes, between dances, the Duke would not even return her to the chairs where Lady Delia and her old friends sat, fanning themselves and sipping champagne. Once he did bring her there, and seated her while he danced with her grandmother. The moment he left her side, a number of men converged upon her, clamoring for the privilege of leading her onto the floor. Tina accepted one of them and found herself being whirled around the floor in a gavotte. At first she was anxious and stiff, but the dedicated skill of her partner soon won her to an appreciation of the lively measure, and she began to enjoy the exercise. When the music ended, she joined in her young partner's laughter as he led her back to the rendezvous.

The Duke was there, frowning coldly.

After that he left her once, to dance with Sally Jersey, and he made sure she was seated beside her grandmother, and drinking fruit punch, before he left.

"John seems particularly devoted tonight," murmured Lady Delia in her ear.

"He is jealous of his consequence," Tina murmured back.

Lady Delia cast a sharp glance at her. "But of course! And he deserves your gratitude for his face-saving stratagem this evening! Even if you were not his fiancée, his action as we greeted Lady Jersey would have saved your credit in Society. It was brilliant!"

Tina nodded agreement.

Although they danced together again, and the Duke squired the two women down to supper with every appearance of enjoyment, the pleasure had gone out of the evening as far as Tina was concerned. She smiled her bright, attractive smile, she widened her great golden eyes upon the Duke's face with every appearance of admiration and delight, she asked questions and made comments in her pretty voice—but all the time she was thinking back to that magical moment on the dance floor, and wondering desolately if she would ever again experience such bliss.

At last the time came to take their leave of their indefatigable hostess. Lady Jersey was still prattling on, her face animated.

"How does she do it?" muttered Lady Delia. "I could swear she hasn't stopped talking all evening."

"She loves it," advised the Duke, also sotto voce. "She talked all through our dance. Eventually I found it rather restful. There is no need to think of something to say."

He and Lady Delia were laughing when it was their turn to thank their hostess and bid her goodnight. Sally Jersey scanned their faces with sharp, interested eyes, then glanced at Tina.

The girl was ready. Instead of looking at Lady Jersey, she had fastened her eyes on the Duke's smiling face in a glance of besotted adoration. Her hostess flashed back to the Duke with reluctant admiration. "How do you manage it?" she mocked. "Another victim—" she glanced at his costume—"to your sword! Goodnight, child," she addressed Tina. "My compliments upon your literary efforts. Although I cannot see Renfrew permitting you to continue with them after your marriage!"

Affably formal, the Duke escorted his ladies out to his carriage, which appeared as by magic on the arrival of the party at the head of the steps. Lady Delia kept a flow of innocuous comment about the costumes, the food, the music, the remarks of her contemporaries, until the carriage pulled up in front of her own well-lighted doorway. As he and a groom assisted her out of the vehicle, she chuckled at the Duke.

"I have just given my celebrated imitation of Sally Jersey! I fear it may be catching!"

Once inside, the Duke bent over her bejewelled hand. "Good-night, Lady Delia. Thank you for being my guest this evening. May I have just two minutes to speak to my fiancée?"

Lady Delia nodded. She looked very tired. "Thank you, John. Yes, you may talk with Tina for a moment—not long, if you please. The evening has been a demanding one for us all."

With that, she left them and walked slowly up the staircase, preceded by her footman with her lighted candle in his hand.

The Duke led Tina to the formal drawing room and closed the door behind them. He escorted her to a chair and almost pushed her down into it.

"Your Grandmother, at least, likes me," he said grimly. "Maybe it takes an older woman to appreciate me."

Staring up in surprise into his discontented face, Tina felt a small surge of hope. Impulsively, meeting the obscure need she sensed in him, she said honestly, "I have never thought of you as *old*! You *must* know that you are—that you have—" Conscious of her self-betrayal, she hesitated.

"If you mean half the things you say, or even one quarter of the things your smile has been implying—*maddeningly*!—all evening, why do you always draw back? Does a man's touch disgust you?"

"Yours does not," answered Tina, throwing her cap over the windmill. "You saw what happened to me tonight when you kissed me."

There was a lightening and softening of the harsh dark features above her. The Duke took her hand and pulled her up to stand close in his embrace. Tina winced at the sudden contact.

The Duke released her at once, his voice grim. "There! You have done it again! Every time—!"

Tina laughed. "Your Grace, when you force a woman against a metal breast-plate as hard as you have just done, it *hurts*! Your knowledge of the female anatomy must tell you what I mean!"

Incredulous, then finally accepting, the Duke only muttered, "I forgot I had the damned thing on!" and joined her laughter.

Very carefully he drew her to him. "This is not a very romantic setting, is it, my little Wisdom? Shall I call tomorrow, wearing a more accomodating garment, and drive you through the park? Yes, that would be *convenable*. We'll take Flora with us. She will be dying of curiosity, and you can enlighten her as we go."

Tina nodded, dreamily content to be held in that light, possessive embrace. Whatever it was he felt for her, she would accept it, and hope that she could someday win his love.

And then his next words shocked her into full awareness.

"We shall continue this absurd engagement until the end of the Season, as I planned," he said casually. "Knowing that you love me will make it all much easier."

She veiled her eyes with suddenly heavy lids. *Oh, God! Do not let him know how this has hurt me!* she thought. She did not fear that she would cry. This agony cut too deep for tears. *Absurd engagement?* Knowing she loved him would make *what* easier?

In a moment, sensing her lassitude, the Duke released her from his embrace. "Tired, little one?" he asked softly. "I shall let you go now. But be ready for our drive out tomorrow! I intend to assert my domination over you while I still can!"

Trying hard to smile, Tina bade him good-night.

Chapter 16

*O*nce in her room, Tina sank onto her bed and shook with the agony of her loss. In one evening she had learned more than she ever wished to know about love and betrayal. The Duke's rejection, so casual, almost gentle, had thrown her into a state of anguish which she did not think she could endure. Tina lifted her head and clasped her trembling hands tightly. She must take action! The Duke had managed to scotch the venomous rumors spread by his sister and his nephew. Lady Jersey had accepted her as a guest. No harm could come to Grandmama, nor even to His Grace, from her innocent forays into Fort Street. And she still had the Purchaser of her manual, who wished further books of increasing difficulty!

Tina clung to that, the one hopeful fact in this tempest of pain. Because it seemed obvious, even to her naïve heart, that the Duke did not intend, and had never intended, to marry her. It was, as he had always stated, a measure of self-protection, pure and simple. The more fool she, for hoping and expecting anything else!

On the other hand, Tina did not believe that she could endure several more weeks of play-acting, of being always at the Duke's side, breathing the fragrance of his immaculately kept body, seeing the powerful beauty of his warm, possessive smile, feeling the hard caress of his hands—and knowing it all to be a sham. It was more, she told herself, than any woman could bear! But what could she do?

Go home. Lady Delia and the Duke could spread the word that her father had been injured. That much was true. And that she had been called back to his bed-side. True, also—and easily to be verified by any scandalmonger. And soon enough he would forget the country bumpkin who had so briefly engaged his attention. The very fact of their supposed engagement would protect him for the rest of the Season. *Oh, why didn't he find some suitable nonentity, and marry her?* cried Tina's sore heart.

Having made her decision, the girl washed her face and began to pack. Within a short time, she had everything ready for the morning, even laying out the travelling dress that she wished to wear. It was one the Duke had commended when he took Flora, Nigel and herself to Astley's one day. She resolved to take that much comfort with her on her flight.

In the event, her departure was less bothersome than she had feared it might be. Lady Delia never came out of her bedroom before noon on mornings after a great ball. The servants, well trained, did not express any of the curiosity they must have felt at seeing Lady Camden's granddaughter embarking in a hackney coach with two large suitcases and a handbag. Dolby, directing the placement of Tina's bags at her feet, ventured one question.

"Milady is aware of your journey, Miss Athena?"

"She knows of my father's accident, Dolby," Tina answered composedly.

"Yes, Miss," agreed the butler, but his glance was full of doubt. Tina smiled at him suddenly. They were *good*, these devoted old servants of Grandmama's! "Thank you for everything," she said, pressing into his reluctant hand the envelopes in which she had placed the vails for the servants. This was such an assurance of her final departure that she had not wished to do it earlier, lest he consult Lady Delia.

She sat back in the coach, the footman closed the door, and the driver set his team into motion. It was goodbye. Tears misted her vision, but she had no desire to look a last time upon Portman Square.

The trip home was not comfortable, even in the mail-coach. She arrived at Malong just before lunchtime the next day, exhausted by the incredible rapidity of the non-stop journey. In the village, she was able to secure the services of a gig and driver from the host of the inn, who bent a pretty forbidding look at her weary, bedraggled state.

"Now, Miss Tina, what's up? Where's yer Grandmama, then?" he demanded with the licence of one who had known her from her childhood.

"I have returned to be with my Papa," said Tina shortly. Old retainers—Joshua Tendon had been head groom in her father's stable until he married the former innkeeper's widow—seemed to think themselves entitled to domineer and pry into one's private affairs! Still, he handed her into the gig with gentle support, and admonished the stable-boy fiercely to get her to Malong Hall safely *or else*!

Her Mama was not too surprised at her arrival, and broke into a paean of thanks for the breeches, which the Duke had apparently dispatched post-haste from London.

"Papa will be up and about within the next few days,"

she volunteered. "His leg is mending nicely, and the—ah—other wounds have healed over. He should be able to resume his normal activities much sooner than he thought. Oh, Tina, it was so good of you to come to us!" Her pretty face under its fetching lace cap clouded. "But I am sure the Duke told us you were going back to London with him! Did you miss him on the road?"

In spite of her weariness, her sore heart, and her natural exasperation at this beloved muddle-head, Tina had to laugh. "Mama, you are a never-failing refreshment to one's spirits! Now let me come in and wash the travel dust from my person, and then perhaps you will instruct Mrs. Morgan to set up a meal for me? I have not eaten in days!"

"This folly of fasting to achieve a fashionable slenderness of figure does not at all please me!" she protested, leading the way up to Tina's old bedroom. "Oh, Morgan!" She caught sight of the elderly housekeeper lurking in the shadows at the rear of the hall. "Here is Miss Tina down from London on that horrid mail-coach, and apparently so eager to rejoin us that she has not stopped to break her fast on the way! Please be so good as to have a collation set up in the morning room. Unless, my love, you would prefer to go *straight* to your bed?" she added, to Tina.

The girl laughed and hugged her. "No, Mama, I'll wash and eat first. It restores me just to be here with you again!"

Her mother, vaguely worried by the sudden arrival, stayed with Tina and escorted her down to the sunny, charming room in which a small table had been set for her. Tucking into the tasty food with relish, Tina soon felt herself much better able to cope with any queries her parent might care to make. But before the inquisition started, she said, "Papa looks quite recovered, does he not? I am glad you did not waken him to greet me when we peeped in just now."

"Dr. Sevenage has given me strict instructions," nodded her mother. "Porter with his luncheon, then a good nap after it. He guarantees that will restore Papa to his old spirits very shortly!"

"I am glad," smiled Tina. "Such a panic as you put me into, with that letter, Mama! *'Death's hall—Death's teeth'!* I had not heard of the new stallion, so you may imagine what I feared!"

Dulcinia had the grace to look ashamed, but it was a temporary guilt. Her pretty face broke into a mischievous smile. "If ever I want your company, I shall know what to do," she said unrepentently.

"You are likely to have a surfeit of it," Tina advised her. "I am home to stay."

At once a frown clouded the pretty face. "But the Duke? Such a lovely man, Tina! I quite lost my heart to him!"

"Be careful, Mama, or I shall tell Papa!" teased the girl, but her heart was not in it. She did not think she could bear an inquisition, however loving, at this moment, so she rose quickly, and dropping a kiss on her Mama's soft cheek, said, "Not another word—not even one syllable, my dear! I am so tired I am ready to drop!" She went into the hallway, ignoring her Mama's loving protests—and ran square into the big hard body of the Duke of Renfrew.

Taken completely by surprise, Tina could not disguise her anxious, loving search of the beloved face. The Duke was weary; hard lines of fatigue grooved his dusty countenance. His eyes also were burning beneath heavy lids.

"Oh, come in and sit down!" begged Tina. "Let me get you something to eat and drink!"

"When I have settled our affairs, you little—" began the Duke in a grating voice totally without affection or tenderness.

Tina flinched automatically.

"Yes, you are wise to prepare yourself, woman!"

the big man snarled at her. "You little coward! What—"

"Your Grace!" piped up Dulcinia happily. "What a *pleasure* to welcome you again to Malong Hall! This silly child was too tired to tell me you were coming. *Morgan!* Send someone to take his Grace up to a bedroom to wash and refresh himself, if you please. Then prepare a meal. The *best* cognac, I think," she dimpled up into the taut, angry face above her.

Slowly the anger and resentment drained out of the dark face. A slow smile took their place, softening the powerful features. "Thank you, Lady Dulcinia! You Long women have a gift for comfort," he glanced slowly over the face and figure of Tina. So intimately searching was his scrutiny that Tina felt herself blushing hotly. The Duke's grin widened. He bowed slightly toward Dulcinia, and then turned to follow the footman up the stairs, halting at the landing to look down at the women who watched his progress from the hallway below. "A gift for comfort," he repeated softly, "as well as the power to enrage a man to madness."

With a final glance at Tina's face, he turned and went on up the stairs.

"What a charming man!" sighed Dulcinia.

"I thought for a moment he was going to beat me," whispered Tina.

"Umphrey often told me he wanted to beat *me*," confided Dulcinia. "I found it very flattering."

Silenced by this startling communication from her parent, Tina went cautiously up to her own room to bathe and change into fresh clothing. In the coming encounter, she would need all the reinforcement available. For there would be an encounter; His Grace's final look had promised it. Tina got out her prettiest dress, a very soft primrose which brought out the gold in her eyes. Dulcinia, who apparently had a very good idea of what her daughter was up to, sent in her own maid to brush and dress Tina's dark hair, and had even sent a tiny pot of rose-pink for her lips and cheeks. This Tina refused, but she did so far arm herself as to dab her finest perfume generously on her person.

"You look good enough to eat, Miss Tina," said the abigail.

Tina shivered involuntarily. "I hope not," she muttered.

And stepped bravely down to the morning room. She was surprised to find the Duke alone, eating heartily.

Catching her glance around the room, the Duke grinned at her. "Your Mama has more *nous* than you, my dear girl. She knows when to make herself scarce!"

This was hardly a promising beginning, thought Tina, warily scanning the beloved face. The predatory smile was much in evidence.

"Why did you . . . come here?" she asked. It embarrassed her when her voice came out in a weak whisper.

The Duke lifted his brandy glass in an insolent salute. "To bring you your voucher to Almack's and—a new contract."

"Contract?" Why did she have to echo his words like some silly ingénue? Tina thought fiercely.

"Yes. It seems the person who purchased your manual wishes to tie you down securely to the production of several more. The terms are adequate."

"You have read my contract?" flared Tina. "By what right—?"

"The right of the Purchaser," said His Grace calmly.

"You—*you* are the Purchaser?" stammered Tina.

The Duke's grin was less threatening. "Yes."

"But why? Why should you want my manuals?"

"I thought Sinclair might have told you."

"Nothing. He said secrecy was the essence of . . . the contract."

The Duke finished his brandy, began to wipe his lips and then desisted, with a devilish glance at the girl. "I am sure you will prefer the flavor of such an excellent brandy to the taste of beer," he said, as a kindly adult promising a treat.

So he was going to kiss her! Tina's knees were attacked by the familiar weakness. She backed away slowly, trembling.

The Duke observed these signs with smug satisfaction. "I see you are suitably impressed by my presence," he taunted. "That is well for you."

He moved forward with the grace of a tiger and took her arm. "Mrs. Morgan tells me that we may use the library for our—conference, since no one but Miss Tina ever goes near the place." He smiled down into her small, worried countenance. "Lead the way, Author."

When they had entered the room, the Duke closed the door firmly after him. "Now, Miss Athena Long, Author, *Seductress*! Why have you chosen to play least-in-sight with me? Why, little coward, did you decide to desert me in the middle of the night, after giving me to believe that we had a bargain?" He strode to her and seized her arms in iron fingers. "*Why?*"

Staring up into those demanding grey eyes, Tina knew that nothing but the truth would serve. "You said our engagement was *absurd*! That knowing I loved you would make it *easier*!" she sobbed with the pain of remembered rejection.

His fingers tightened. "But of course it was absurd! The melodramatics of the scene in my library with the Pennets! Your naïve stratagem 'to save my bacon'! Would you not call *that* Cheltenham rodomontade of the most ridiculous? And as a sensible female, why did you not confront me with your—your suspicions at once?"

Tina drew a shuddering breath. "I suppose because I am not—a sensible female," she said. "Thinking as I did, I could not bear to be with you for weeks, close to you every day—"

The Duke's voice interrupted sharply, "You find me so distasteful?"

"Oh, *no!*" She looked up and saw the pain in his face; her heart was wrung. "How could you think that, John, when you saw how your kiss affected me? I could not bear to pretend that we were to marry, when it was all a sham! Too painful—for one who loves you," she ended bravely.

The Duke's hands closed more tightly upon her arms. She looked into his face. "I did not wish you to feel obligated to me," she confessed, "but the most urgent thing was that I really couldn't stand the pain of seeing you—and not—having you!"

The Duke drew a hard breath. "And *I* thought my advanced age and experience revolted you. I feared I could not make you happy."

Tina dared a tentative smile. "*That* is absurd, Your Grace!"

"You called me John just now," the Duke reminded her.

"John! You know how you affect me! You teased me about it!"

"Did I?" queried the Duke, with less assurance than he had ever displayed toward her.

Tina, looking at the Duke's handsome face with the eyes of love, perceived something she had not seen before. Under the arrogant facade of the dark corsair, beneath the imperturbable front which His Grace usually presented to his world, there breathed a man of passion—and sensitivity. A man who could be disappointed, hurt, betrayed. Tina's warm heart swelled with compassion and love. She knew he would not be able to accept the full measure of what she felt for him—not yet! But her keen woman's mind began to see the answer. With a long, loving, teasing look into that guarded yet vulnerable countenance, she said, "Of course you did! A man of your knowledge of the world! Your experience! Surely you would know when a woman is in love with you!"

"Perhaps I saw it as mere physical attraction, or . . . pity?" His voice was a little stronger, more assured, and his grasp on her arms even tighter. Tina shook with inner joy, but her voice was still gaily teasing as she challenged,

"*Perhaps* you are a wily devil, John Alexander Stone! What rig are you up to? You know I *adore* you, every virile, desirable inch of you—and there are plenty of them!" She pulled back a little, to observe the effect of her remarks. He was staring intently into her small, enchanting face, seeking the reassurance he needed.

"I believe I must always call you Alexander! The world may see you as Duke John, but to me you are the Conqueror. You *bestride the narrow world* of Polite Society *like a Colossus*," she primmed her lovely mouth, miming pedantry, "as Shakespeare said of Caesar," then broke the illusion with laughter. "In fact, sir," she was quaking inwardly now with terrified delight at the expression which blazed on the Duke's face, "As Milton said, '*Your*—er—dark *large front and eye sublime declare Absolute rule.*'"

Slowly, purposefully, the big warm hands left her arms and found their way around her slender body. Then hard fingers turned her chin up so her eyes were compelled to meet his own.

"Little minx! I—I—" Still he could not express the feelings, so new to him, which were shaking and changing him. He took a deep breath and, put his lips, as hard and warm as his hands, over Tina's, possessing them, ravishing them, adoring them. After a timeless moment he drew away, and touched her face with gentle fingers. He attempted a casual smile. "I am glad," said His Grace the Duke of Renfrew, "that I chose a literary female to marry. It will make it easier for you to tell me how wonderful I am." He pulled her even closer to his powerful body. With temerity and love, Tina clutched him with her arms and hugged him hard.

"Oh, yes, darling Alexander, yes!"

The Duke essayed a laugh. "I shall expect to hear it at least once a day for the rest of our lives! Is it a bargain?"

"It is a bargain," agreed Tina joyously, "so long as you pay me every day with one of those earth-shaking kisses of yours."

His shout of laughter, so free, so delighted, eased the tension between them. "Only *one*? Paltry!" he teased happily. "One kiss *per diem* will satisfy you?" He hugged her until she thought her ribs would crack, but Tina voiced no objection. "I shall have something to say about that! I cannot have it rumored that I am clutch fisted with my wife! *Close armed*, yes!" he grinned wolfishly. "Oh, be assured, my Athena, there will be more than one kiss a day—*much* more!" He gave her a sample which left her limp and loving in his arms.

She had never seen such open happiness in her dark corsair's face.

He smiled down at her, himself unaware of how revealing that smile was. "I have brought you a few wedding gifts, my little Bluestocking." He swung her up into his arms and carried her over to a deep leather chair, where he held her on his lap. "First, the reason I need your wonderful manuals. I am establishing schools in the villages near to each of my estates. The schools will be free for the children of farmers, shop-keepers, servants—in short, for anyone who wishes to enroll. And you shall write all the manuals and train the teachers to pass on to the students your own joyous pleasure in learning." He kissed her again, lingeringly, possessively, before she could express her thanks, leaving her breathless and dizzy with delight.

He observed her reaction with satisfaction, taking in the soft rosy blush, the wide dazzled golden eyes, the soft breath coming quickly between swollen lips. "You really do enjoy being kissed by me, do you not, my Athena?"

The girl met his gaze honestly. "Better than any gift you could give me," she averred.

"Better than a wedding ring? Or a diamond necklace? I'll give you those, too. I am besotted with you, my darling girl: *You are sure I am not too old for you?*" he whispered ardently against her soft mouth.

"Age is only a number," she said softly. "You are everything I could ever want—more than I ever dreamed a man could be! As long as you love me, neither of us need ever fear the years."

Her lover held her close to his heart. Time became timeless in that quiet room where Tina's dreams, wonderful as they had been, had never reached the warm delight of this reality.

He watched her with hungry eyes, this once-arrogant, cold-hearted man who had never trusted any woman. He took in the rosy blush, the wide, dazzled golden eyes, the breath coming quickly between her parted lips. "You really do enjoy being kissed by me, do you not, my Athena?"

The girl met his gaze honestly. "Better than any gift you could give me," she averred.

"Better than a diamond necklace?" he teased, to hide his incredulous joy. "I have one for you."

"An impressive bauble," the girl admitted, her eyes adoring him.

He laughed. "You little innocent, you couldn't care less! But a wedding ring? I have that for you, too."

Tina caught her breath. "Are you sure you really wish to be married to me?" she whispered.

The Duke in turn whispered ardently against her soft mouth, "I am besotted with you, my darling girl! Are *you* sure I am not too old for you?"

She drew back in his embrace, looked into his eyes and said clearly, "You are everything I could ever want—more than I ever dreamed a man could be!"

He caught her close to him again. *"I love you,"* he said, like a promise, like a prayer. "For all our lives—and beyond!"

And Tina, her heart on her lips, knew that her dreams had come true.